RESTRAINT

STINGRAYS HOCKEY
BOOK 1

MARI CARR

RESTRAINT

Girlfriend…without benefits?

Hometown hockey hero, Blake has life completely figured out. He's footloose and fancy free with the world's coolest job and an endless parade of puck bunnies ready to help him celebrate his victories. The status quo is working for him, so why does he agree to co-parent a stray puppy with his too-serious, workaholic neighbor, Erika? And why is he so annoyed when she suddenly starts dating some tool named Doug? And why can't he stop finding excuses to see her and touch her and kiss her and… She's not his girlfriend, right?

Erika has enough on her plate as an ER doctor without adding any more stress to her life. So adopting a dog with Blake, the fun-loving, never-take-anything-serious, commitment-phobe across the hall is a stupid idea, right? Of course, she also probably shouldn't be his plus-one for charity galas either. Or seeking comfort from him during a thunderstorm. Or kissing his five-for-fighting boo-boos better. Or letting him teach her how to "reduce stress" with her personal toy collection. After all, he's not her boyfriend. Is he?

So what happens when two people reluctant to commit find love where they least expect it… Right across the hall.

CHAPTER ONE

"IT'S SOOOO EARLY."

"Babe," Blake Wright drawled unapologetically. "I told you last night. I've got a bunch of errands to run this morning before practice."

Mindy gave him what he assumed was supposed to be a cute pouty face, but it fell short. Probably because her blouse was wrinkled, her blonde hair was frizzy on one side of her head, plastered flat to the other, and last night's mascara was smeared around her eyes, making her look like a raccoon.

They'd engaged in one hell of a celebration dance, he thought with pride. Mindy had even enlivened things, entertaining him with what she called her private party trick. The woman could actually tie herself up in bed.

Last night, he'd thought it was funny because he was high on life and the win. This morning, as he recalled her special skill, he wasn't sure if he was impressed or horrified…because number one, why? And number two…

No, no number two.

Just why?

He gave her a quick kiss, one that she attempted to prolong

by wrapping her arms around his neck, but Blake pried them off, trying not to let it annoy him.

They always had a good time in the sack, but the last few times Mindy had stayed over, he'd found her dragging out the morning-after goodbyes. The two of them weren't in a relationship because he'd made it very clear, right from the beginning, that he wasn't looking for a girlfriend. Mindy, one of the Baltimore Stingrays' most loyal puck bunnies, had assured him she was cool with the occasional "victory" hookup.

"Let's go back to bed," she purred.

He shook his head. "No can do."

"I'll make it worth your while," she added, drawing a long hot-pink fingernail down the center of his chest. He hadn't bothered to put on a shirt before walking her to the door, just tugging on a pair of lounge pants instead.

"Mindy," he said, hoping she heard the tone of warning in his voice. Back at the beginning, she'd been the perfect hookup— hot sex, followed by a sound sleep and quick goodbye in the morning, then Blake didn't see her again until the next time the Stingrays won.

Before Mindy could persist—and he could tell she was going to—he was saved by a new voice.

"Looks like the Rays won last night."

Blake grinned, looking up just as his neighbor, Dr. Erika Nelson, hit the top stair to their shared floor. He and Erika lived across the hall from each other in a luxury apartment building near Charm City, in Southeast Baltimore. While they lived on the fourth floor, and there was an elevator, Erika insisted on using the stairs more often than not.

She was obviously returning from her morning jog, her chestnut-brown hair pulled back in a ponytail, her skin shimmering with a slight sheen of sweat.

"You didn't watch the game?" he asked in surprise. One of the first things he'd done after Erika moved in was convert her not only to hockey but to the Stingrays specifically. She was now one of their team's biggest fans.

Erika grimaced. "Worked the late shift in the ER. I'll have to catch the highlights on TV at some point today."

He crossed his arms as he leaned against the doorframe. "Spoiler alert. We kicked Carolina's ass."

"Poor Carolina," Erika joked. "What did she ever do to you?"

Mindy's brows furrowed. "He means the hockey team."

Erika bit her lip—probably to keep herself from laughing—then said, "Oh, right. Of course. How silly of me." She unzipped a pocket in her jacket, digging around for her apartment key.

"Hopping night in the ER?" he asked.

Erika blew out a tired sigh. "Always."

"Anything interesting?" Blake had become a bit obsessed with hearing Erika's work stories. As an ER doctor at Hopkins, God knew the woman had treated some interesting—and hilarious—cases.

Like the woman who'd broken her foot putting on skinny jeans by jumping up and down, or the couple who'd lost a condom during sex that Erika had to fish out of the mortified woman, or the guy who'd hooked his own eyelid while practicing casting in his living room.

"Nope. Last night was a potpourri of the classics—chest pain, skin infections, and dehydration from the flu. I did have to put ten stitches in a kid's forehead after he fell off his bunkbed. The kid was fine, but the poor dad was *not* okay with the blood. He vomited all over himself while driving his son to the hospital. The smell was ungodly. Apparently, they'd had jambalaya for dinner."

Blake laughed, but Mindy made a face and started to gag.

"That's disgusting," she said.

Blake pushed off the door, ready for Mindy to leave. Erika didn't need any more ammo when it came to Mindy's lacking sense of humor *or* intelligence. He'd pointed out on countless occasions that he wasn't fucking her because of her brains, but that didn't stop Erika from doing a dead-on impersonation of the dim-witted woman just to give him a hard time.

"Well, thanks for a great evening, Mindy," he said, moving her away from his apartment, ready to send her on her merry way.

Mindy turned like she was going to go for one more kiss, but he dodged it, placing his hand on her back to guide her toward the stairs.

"Okay, then," she grumbled, unhappy at his hasty dismissal. He was going to have to reconsider their standing arrangement and start calling someone else for his post-game celebratory booty calls. Mindy's goals for their association clearly no longer matched his.

"Bye, Mindy," Erika said cheerfully.

"Bye, Eileen."

Blake stifled a groan. Erika had introduced herself several times, but Mindy seemed utterly incapable of remembering her name.

Mindy headed down the stairs as Blake continued toward Erika, who started singing "Come On Eileen," as she opened her apartment door and walked inside.

"Toora loora toora loo-rye-aye," Erika belted out.

"Smart-ass," he muttered, even as the tune starting playing in his head. Great. Nothing like an earworm. He knew what he was going to be singing all day.

Blake followed her, heading straight for her fancy Nespresso machine. Grabbing a cup from the cupboard and a pod from the container on the counter, he fired it up as she toed off her tennis shoes.

"I'm going to have to start a coffee fund if you keep coming over here and helping yourself," she said, the threat nowhere near new. "Those pods aren't cheap. It's why I limit myself to one cup a day."

"Bill me," he teased, opening the refrigerator to grab the creamer. "And how many times do I have to tell you? Life is too short to put limits on yourself. You like fancy coffee with the foam on top, so you should just have it. Why mess around with the shit you don't enjoy as much?"

Erika grabbed a bottle of water from the counter and took a long swig. "You know what your problem is?"

He didn't bother to prompt her for a response, since past experience told him she was going to tell him anyway.

He and Erika had been neighbors for three years, and during that time, she'd somehow become his best friend, his sometime nemesis, and that nagging voice in the back of his head—some people called it a conscience—all rolled into one.

Erika put the cap back on the water bottle and pointed it at him. "You have no restraint. You see something, you take it."

He waited for her to get to the problem. When she stopped talking, he snorted. "That's not a problem. That's called a happy lifestyle. The opposite would be *yours*, where you deny yourself pleasure for the sake of self-control. Total waste."

"Yes, but sometimes you grab things that aren't exactly good for you."

"Are you talking about Mindy? Because I can assure you, last night...she was very, very good for me."

She huffed out a breath. "One of these days, you might want to try to start thinking with the head on your shoulders as opposed to the one in your pants."

He didn't bother continuing the argument because at the moment, it didn't feel like one he could win. "So you really didn't watch any of the game last night?"

"Didn't need to," she said with a mischievous grin. "I watch you score enough here without having to tune in."

He laughed and debated denying her claim. While he indulged in the occasional celebratory fuck after home games with Mindy and a couple other women, he wouldn't define himself as an outright playboy. That name more accurately described his best friend and teammate, Zac Phillips, aka Tank.

Tank's bedroom door really should be the revolving type, just to save him time.

Like Tank, Blake wasn't interested in a committed relationship, but that didn't mean he was fucking his way through the female population of Baltimore either. Erika wasn't wrong when she said he scored a lot, but the truth was, he limited his booty calls to the same three or four women.

"I wish you could have come last night. We were on fire."

"I turned on the TVs in the waiting room and breakroom to the game," Erika confessed. "I caught snippets during downtimes, but not as much as I would have liked."

Blake offered Erika free tickets to every home game. Unfortunately, his neighbor was in the last year of her residency at Hopkins, something she took very seriously. She was a workaholic, which probably wasn't a bad thing, considering her chosen career path, because there wasn't a more dedicated doctor in the city. And since she was focusing on emergency medicine, her hours weren't limited to nine to five, like family practice physicians. It wasn't unusual for her to work the night shift, and depending on the traffic in the emergency room, there were many times when she worked longer than her scheduled hours.

"Next time," she said, crossing her fingers. "Hopefully."

He pointed at her. "I'm holding you to that." He returned to the refrigerator, opening the door and peering inside. "Because you missed a scorcher last night. I scored twice."

"Wow. Mindy really goes the extra mile, doesn't she?"

He glanced over his shoulder, rolling his eyes, and then decided to hell with it. She was having too much fun at his expense. Time to give some back. "Twice on the ice. Three times in bed. Mindy's the Energizer bunny."

"TMI, hotshot."

"Remind me again, Doc. When was the last time *you* scored?"

"On the ice? Never."

Blake leaned back into the fridge. "Always denying yourself." He shook his head, tutting in disappointment. "And it's not just sex. Where the hell is your food? Because it looks to me like you're living on condiments."

Erika drifted around the counter until she stood behind him, peering into the refrigerator as well. "There's yogurt in there."

He rose, closing the door and crossing his arms. While Erika liked to give him shit about his casual hookups, Blake tended to return the favor when it came to her complete inability to feed herself properly.

"Erik. I thought you were going to start using Instacart, since you hate going to the grocery store."

She sighed, no longer calling him to task over his nickname for her. The first few hundred times he'd called her Erik, she'd attempted to correct him. Nowadays, he got the sense she liked the name, though God knew she'd never admit it.

"I have a cart half built," she said. "Just haven't managed to finish it and place the order."

"What are you eating for dinner?" he asked.

"I've been on nights this week. So I grab something from the vending machine or takeout from one of the restaurants in the hospital."

Blake shook his head but didn't bother issuing his standard lecture. It would be wasted breath. "I've got bacon and eggs at my place. I can make us some breakfast."

Erika perked up at the sound of bacon. "Awesome. Let me grab a shower real quick and I'll meet you back at your place in ten. I'll bring the yogurt over to contribute to the meal."

He grinned. "Great, but I get the blueberry."

"That's my fav—" She stopped, then sighed. "Fine. I'll eat the peach," she grumbled.

Blake left her apartment, crossed the hall to his place, and started to tidy. He wasn't a messy guy, per se, but he also had a tendency to treat his living room like an extension of his closet.

He grabbed a jacket off the floor and hung it up, then grabbed the two pairs of shoes from the living room floor and tossed them into his bedroom. He'd strip the sheets after breakfast and get a load of laundry going.

Blake wouldn't call himself a neat freak, but he also wasn't a slob like Tank. He kept his apartment tidy, and he paid a woman to come in once a week to clean. It was the same housekeeper Erika used because, like him, she liked a clean house but didn't have the time—or the desire—to do it herself.

Grabbing a frying pan from the cabinet, he pulled the ingredients he needed from the refrigerator, scrambling half a dozen eggs while the bacon cooked. He checked his messages once the eggs were in another pan. There were a couple texts from Tank, asking if he wanted to go out for a drink after practice today, and one from the assistant coach with some general information regarding their next road trip. They were flying to the West Coast the day after tomorrow for three nights.

The regular season had just begun, last night the first regulation game following two weeks of preseason. Winning the first game felt like a good omen to him, especially since they'd gotten knocked out of playoffs at the end of last season. He was looking forward to getting back into the swing of things.

He'd been playing for the Baltimore Stingrays the past four years, traded to his hometown team after six years with San Jose. While he'd enjoyed his time in California, there was nothing like coming home and playing for his dream team. He'd grown up worshiping the Rays, swearing to anyone who would listen that one day, he was going to be playing in the Baltimore arena and wearing the blue-and-white jersey.

There's nothing like a dream come true, and that was what he'd been living the past four years. Initially, he'd shared an apartment with Tank, his new teammate offering the room vacated by another player who'd been traded to Vegas. While he and Tank were truly the best of friends, it hadn't taken them long to figure out that friendship wasn't going to survive if they remained roommates.

So three years ago, he'd moved into this apartment, and a

month after he'd settled in, Erika took up residence in the place across the hall. He'd flirted with her pretty hot and heavy the first few months because, one, flirting was second nature to him, and two, Erika was a natural beauty. However, she'd rebuffed every single one of his advances.

Blake didn't consider himself a cocky guy, but her continued refusals had started to sting, simply because he wasn't used to being rejected.

Finally, he'd point-blank asked her why she wouldn't go out with him, and Erika—who always shot straight—told him she wasn't about to shit where she ate. She'd asked what he was looking for, and when he confessed he wasn't interested in a serious relationship, she'd informed him that was *exactly* what she wanted…someday. Casual sex wasn't her thing, so when she was ready to hop back into the dating pool—after her residency was over—she'd be looking for a prospective husband, not a one-night stand.

Since the H word gave him hives, he backed off on the flirting.

Erika successfully convinced him the two of them would be better off as friends, since they both loved their apartments and planned to stay there for the foreseeable future. When she pointed out how awkward it would be to run into each other after hooking up, he realized she was right.

Since then, they hadn't just become friends. They'd become best friends, and he was glad he hadn't pushed her for a hookup. She was an important part of his life, and their current relationship was perfect.

Blake had just finished plating the food when the door to his apartment opened and Erika walked in. Knocking was a thing of the past for the two of them.

"Smells delicious," she said, as she placed the two yogurt cups on the counter next to the plates. They each claimed a tall stool, digging into their breakfasts with gusto.

Once they'd eaten, Erika leaned back and sighed contentedly.

"That was so good. Thanks, Blake. I was this close," she pressed her forefinger and thumb together, "to stopping on the way back from my run for a donut."

"Why didn't you?" he asked. "Next time that urge hits, bring me back a Boston creme."

She shook her head. "Nope. No point in running if I just shove all the calories I burned right back in."

Blake rolled his eyes. "More denying yourself happiness."

He didn't bother to add that a donut wasn't going to hurt her. Erika was health-conscious, and there weren't too many days when she didn't manage to work in some form of exercise—either in the form of a jog or on the nautilus equipment in their building's gym. Blake joined her to work out on occasion—more often during the off-season—and she always gave him a run for his money.

"Pizza night here next Monday. You in?" Blake had invited a bunch of his teammates over, and every single one had asked if Erika would be there. The guys were as fond of his neighbor as he was.

For some reason, his apartment had become the "dinner" gathering place, and Erika likened their group to the *Big Bang Theory* friends, as they avoided sitting around a proper table, opting instead to gather around the coffee table with their plates on their laps.

"Do you even have to ask?"

He frowned when he spied dark circles under her eyes that he hadn't noticed earlier. "You look tired."

She shrugged. "I didn't want to say anything in front of Mindy, but I treated two gunshot wounds last night."

Unfortunately, Erika was no stranger to violence. Baltimore, while not quite the crime capital it had been a decade ago, still saw way too much violence in terms of gang activity.

"Did they make it?"

She nodded. "Yeah, but one guy is facing a long road to

recovery. I swear I'll never understand why people feel the need to unalive other people. And it's always over something stupid."

Blake felt the same way. "What were these guys fighting about? Drugs or gang pride?"

"Drugs. Lately, it's always drugs," she replied, glancing toward his fridge. He kept each month's game schedule tacked there. "Heading to the West Coast this week, huh?"

"Yeah. I'll be gone three nights, so pull out your phone, Doc."

She gave him a curious look but did as he asked. "Why?"

"Because I'm not going to be here to feed you. Pull up the Instacart app." It wasn't unusual for them to have dinner, either alone or with some of his teammates, three or four nights a week. During the season, it was less; off-season, it was more.

Usually they did takeout or delivery, but sometimes he cooked. Blake enjoyed cooking, while Erika viewed it with the same disdain some people felt for a trip to the dentist.

She grinned as she clicked on the Instacart app. He leaned close to her, pointing out a few things she should add to her cart. Because Erika wasn't much of a cook—though that had less to do with skill and more to do with lack of desire—he watched as she added simple fare, like cans of soup and premade salads.

"Get a loaf of bread, some cheese, and turkey too," he suggested. "Sandwiches are easy to make. You can take them to work. I'm sure they're probably healthier than anything you're getting out of that vending machine."

She nodded, adding the items to her cart. "That's a good idea."

Even though she was agreeing, Blake was eighty percent positive the meat would go bad before she ever remembered to make a sandwich. Erika was a total enigma. The woman was incredibly intelligent and extremely empathetic. He didn't doubt for a second that she had a great bedside manner. However, her ability to take care of others didn't translate when it came to taking care of herself, which was why Blake found himself in the position of reminding her to eat more often than not.

"Okay," he said, once he was satisfied she'd added enough food to her cart to get her through the next few days. "Now, check out."

It seemed like a no-brainer, but he'd helped her build carts before only to discover she'd never placed the damn order.

She snickered, then checked out, flashing the screen when she was finished to show him she'd done as he asked. "Happy?"

He nodded. "Yep. But I'd be even happier if you remembered to eat the food without me here to tell you."

Erika winked playfully. "I like to give your life meaning."

He snorted. "I have a very full life, thank you very much. Think about it, Erik. We've both got it made. Great apartments, friends, dream jobs. What the hell else could we want?"

She shrugged. "I don't know. You don't wonder sometimes if something is missing?"

He could tell it was a serious question, but he wasn't sure how to answer it. The truth was, he didn't think anything was missing, but something about her tone told him *she* did. "What could be missing?"

Erika fell silent long enough that he didn't think she was going to answer. "I don't know."

She *did* know, but she wasn't saying. So he said what she wasn't. "You mean a relationship, don't you?"

She shrugged one shoulder, then nodded. "Yeah. I guess I do. Sometimes, I feel…lonely."

Her confession took Blake by surprise because he would have thought Erika was as happy with her life as he was with his. "Really?"

"You don't ever feel that way?"

He shook his head. "Not at all. I mean, I'm always surrounded by people—fans, friends, teammates. When the hell would I get lonely?"

She sighed, then shrugged off the conversation. "True."

"Besides, I thought you were putting romance on the back burner until your residency was over."

"I'm in the last year, and Hopkins has already hired me to continue on. For the first time in a decade, I feel settled. But you're right. I *am* happy. I'm not sure why I'm in a funk, but it'll pass. Sorry I brought it up." She changed the subject before he could press her for more. "No game tonight?"

He let her get away with dropping the relationship talk. It wasn't like he could offer her any advice, anyway. He avoided relationships like the plague and, unlike her, he didn't feel the pull to seek more than what he already had. "Just an afternoon practice."

"Guess that means no Mindy."

Blake grinned. "You know the rule. Sex is my reward for scoring a goal and winning a game."

"Thought you didn't believe in denying yourself?"

Blake reached out and ruffled her damp hair. "You're batting a thousand today on the smart-ass scale."

Erika ducked out of his reach. "What if the team wins, but you don't score?"

"No sex, because I didn't do my part."

"What if you score a goal, but the team loses?"

"No sex, because I obviously didn't score enough goals."

She tilted her head. "You're weird."

He laughed. "Nope. I just like to feel like I've earned my reward."

"Mindy," she said, crinkling her nose, making it clear she didn't consider that much of a reward.

"Or Paulette or Lara."

She flipped her hair over her shoulder. "I don't see them as often as I do Mindy."

Blake considered that, and he knew why. Mindy knew his rules for victory sex, and she appeared to have him on speed dial whenever the parameters were met. He'd had a text from her asking if he wanted to "meet" before he'd even made it back to the locker room after the game last night.

Next time, he'd ignore her texts and give Paulette or Lara a call. Regularly sleeping with Mindy had obviously given the woman the wrong idea.

"What can I say? Mindy's an enthusiastic fan who knows how to celebrate in style," he joked, wiggling his eyebrows.

Erika put her finger in her mouth, pretending to gag.

"At least I'm getting some action, Doc."

"Not this again," she said, throwing her hands up. "You have an unhealthy interest in my sex life."

"You'd have to have one for that to be true."

"Unlike you, Balakay," she said, pronouncing his name like the substitute teacher in the old Key and Peele skit, "I prefer to keep certain aspects of my life private. For all you know, I could have a very active sex life."

"Bullshit," he fake coughed. He had the same bird's-eye view of her front door that she had of his. As such, he knew perfectly well she hadn't hosted a single sleepover since moving in three years ago…at least not when he was in town. She'd gone on a handful of dates, mainly with men she knew from work, but as far as he could tell, none of the guys she'd gone out with had ever made it past the good-night kiss—and he couldn't recall any of them progressing to a second date.

"You know, maybe you wouldn't be so focused on the sex aspect of your relationship if you actually tried to develop something deeper and more meaningful yourself."

Blake frowned, shooting her a horrified look. "Thought you knew better than to use the R word with me, Erik."

Erika snorted. "Thought it was the H word I was supposed to avoid."

He pretended to start scratching like he had a rash. "They're both deadly."

"Idiot," she muttered.

"Listen, Doc. I'm not swearing off the R or H words forever, but you have to think practically. It wouldn't be fair to take myself off the market when I'm still so young and hot."

She quirked one eyebrow, and he braced himself for an

insult. "I'm not sure you and I define 'young and hot' the same way."

He hip-bumped her, a silent kudos for her joke.

"So you might get married someday?" she asked. "I always got the impression that was a hard no for you."

"It's just not in my immediate plans for the future, but somewhere down the line, who knows? Right now, I'm focusing on my career, on setting all the records," he added with a cocky grin.

"Would those records be on the ice or in your bedroom? Because you have to be creeping up on some sort of record for most—"

"On the ice," he interjected, putting them back on track. "There's plenty of time for boring shit like settling down with the old ball and chain when I'm in my fifties."

Erika laughed. "Thank you so much for reminding me why I was smart to turn down all your invitations to," she finger-quoted several of her next words, "'date' you when you first moved in. I've since learned 'dating' to you is actually synonymous for 'hooking up.'"

"Semantics," he teased.

Erika rose, shaking her head in amusement. "Well, I'm going to head back over to my place. Laundry beckons."

Blake stood too. "Same. Plus, I've got a bunch of errands to run before practice." He walked her to the door.

"Thanks for breakfast," she said, with a wave.

He smiled, then watched as she crossed the hall, disappearing into her own apartment before closing the door. He leaned against the frame for a minute, considering Erika's confession about feeling lonely.

She'd surprised him. Mostly because, try as he may, he couldn't understand or relate.

He had a good life. The life he wanted. He was a lucky guy, and he knew it.

"Not a thing missing," he murmured to himself, smiling as

he headed to the bedroom to strip the sheets. "Not a damn thing."

CHAPTER TWO

ERIKA SMILED when she walked into the waiting room and saw Blake waiting for her, leaning on the receptionist's counter and flirting with one of the nurses, Denise.

He waved when he spotted her, straightening to join her. "Hey, Doc. Ready to go?"

She nodded. "Sure am. I appreciate you picking me up."

"No reason to take an Uber when I was heading home at the same time."

She'd mentioned grabbing an Uber this morning when she told him her car was in the shop. Blake had insisted on coming to get her instead, since her shift ended an hour after his game.

"The timing *was* pretty perfect," she acknowledged with a grin. "Getting to work wasn't a big deal since I don't mind walking during the day, and the weather was lovely, but it's a different story at night."

The area around Hopkins wasn't the kind of place a woman wanted to roam alone after dark. Baltimore was one of those cities where a person could feel perfectly safe walking one block, then two blocks later, be terrified out of their minds.

"I definitely wouldn't let you walk home after dark. I'm happy to pick you up."

Erika glanced at the sky when they walked out of the emergency room. "I thought it was calling for rain."

"It still is, but I think it's starting later than they forecasted." They made their way to the parking garage, where he'd parked his car.

"Well, I owe you one for this. And don't worry, it'll be business as usual tomorrow because the mechanic called, and my car is ready." She'd finally made an appointment to have her car looked at after dealing with a weird pinging noise for nearly a month.

"Did they figure out what was wrong with it?" Blake asked.

She nodded. "Yeah, something to do with a loose exhaust bracket. Whatever the hell that means. God only knows what it's going to cost me."

"Hopefully it won't be too bad. Did you go to Rocky's like I suggested?"

She nodded.

"Good. He'll take care of you. Rocky's an anomaly. An honest mechanic."

She smiled. "Glad to hear it. Soooo…coming to get me didn't ruin any horizontal victory dance plans tonight, did it? Or is Mindy meeting you back at your place?"

He shook his head, grimacing. "Unfortunately, no dancing. We got our asses handed to us."

"Oh. I'm sorry." Erika knew how much her competitive neighbor hated to lose.

"Not sure why it was such a slog tonight. We couldn't get into any sort of rhythm. Nothing—and I mean *nothing*—would hit the back of the net."

"Maybe it was jet lag from the West Coast trip," she suggested. "You got back pretty late the night before last. I'm sure that had to take a toll on you guys."

"Yeah, Coulton said the same thing." Coulton Moore was the Rays' goalie, a gentle giant if Erika had ever met one.

"I don't know how you manage as well as you do," Erika

added. "Hopping back and forth across the country with precious little time between games sounds exhausting to me."

Blake pulled his keys out of his pocket and hit the fob, the car lights flashing as the doors unlocked. "It's part of the job, and you get used to it after a while. We're usually better at bouncing back from the travel. Tonight, we were just off."

"You'll win the next one." Erika climbed into the passenger seat as Blake slid behind the steering wheel. She leaned her head back and sighed, glad to finally be off her feet.

Blake started the car but didn't put it in gear as he studied her face. "Doesn't look like your night was any better than mine."

She rubbed her eyes wearily. "I'd have to check the latest census, but I'm fairly certain I treated fifty percent of the population of Baltimore tonight. There's a nasty stomach virus going around, and we currently live in a city filled with dehydrated people."

"Shit. Hope you don't get sick. Hell, I hope *I* don't get sick," he added with a grin. "Sold-out game tonight. Lot of people breathing the same air."

"You're healthy as a horse." She tried to recall if she could remember a time when Blake was ever sick. She couldn't even recall him getting a cold. It was one of the things the two of them had in common. Erika could count on one hand the number of times she'd been sick in bed. And most of those were when she was a kid. "I wore my mask the entire time. Plus, my immune system is probably the strongest part of me. God knows it's always getting a workout." She sighed again, slipping off one of her shoes, rubbing her aching foot. "It's good to be off my feet. I didn't sit down once tonight."

Blake reached across the console and grasped her knee, giving it a squeeze. "You know, I could use a beer. What do you say we stop into Pat's Pub and unwind with a pint before heading back?"

It was late, but Erika was too wired to sleep. "That's sounds great. I didn't have time for more than a handful of crackers on my break, so I might grab a sandwich too."

Blake pierced her with a look. The one that told her he was probably going to give her yet another speech about how she should take better care of herself.

"I packed a sandwich," she said in her defense. "I just didn't have time to eat it."

Blake scoffed. "Yeah. Like that makes it better. You're allowed meal breaks, Dr. Nelson."

She shrugged but didn't reply because him giving her a lecture wasn't going to change the fact she would always work through her breaks if she knew someone was suffering in the waiting room. Blake knew that too, but it didn't stop him from trying anyway. He was a good friend that way.

He took a left at the next light, the two of them heading toward one of the local pubs near their neighborhood. They drove in a companionable silence, comfortable enough with each other to get lost in their own thoughts.

After parallel parking in a spot near the pub, Blake circled the car, offering her a hand to help her out of his Audi. He chuckled at her exaggerated groan as she got out.

"It's not that low," he said, replying to her unspoken complaint.

"It's like I'm sitting on the ground."

They walked into the pub together, Blake's hand resting at the small of her back.

"Blake, Erika," Padraig, the bartender, called out from behind the bar, offering a wave.

Blake had introduced her to Pat's Pub a few months after she'd moved into their building, the local watering hole a favorite of the team. Blake and his teammates did a lot of celebrating in the place, as Padraig and his dad, Tristan, two of the biggest Stingrays fans on the planet, always rolled out the red carpet after big wins.

"Hey, Padraig," Blake called out. "Good to see you, man. It's been a while."

The bartender walked out from behind the counter to join them, shaking Blake's hand. "Wasn't expecting to see you tonight. Tank said you'd opted out on the 'drowning your sorrows' portion of the evening. Tough loss, by the way."

"Thanks. Not our finest moment." She watched as Blake glanced around the pub. "I actually forgot a few of the guys were planning to come by. Tank insisted he needed to drink away the agony of defeat."

"Well, he's putting a dent in it," Padraig joked.

Glancing toward the back of the pub, she spotted Tank, Coulton, and a couple other Rays players holding court with a bunch of puck bunnies—including Mindy.

"Want to go say hello?" Erika offered half-heartedly. She'd been looking forward to a quiet meal. Hanging out with a bunch of his teammates and the giggly groupies who seemed to follow them everywhere they went would classify as anything but.

Blake shook his head. "No. I just left those guys. Besides, Mindy would probably latch on, and I don't have the energy for her tonight. We'll say goodbye on our way out."

She smiled, relieved, though somewhat surprised he was trying to avoid Mindy.

"Erika had a busy night at the hospital, so we thought we'd stop in for a pint and a bite," Blake explained as he let Padraig guide them to a booth in a quiet corner near the front of the bar, well away from the group in the back, who mercifully hadn't noticed their arrival.

"How's this?" Padraig asked about the table.

"Perfect," Erika said, taking the menu Padraig handed her. "Did you eat dinner yet?" she asked Blake.

"Had something a few hours before the game, but nothing since. So, I'm starving." Blake typically ate three hours before the puck drop, and usually the same thing—chicken breast or some other lean protein, rice, and green veggies. He took his pre-game routines very seriously.

Blake ordered them each a pint of Guinness, and Padraig headed back to the bar to get their drinks while they perused the menus.

"What looks good?" Blake asked, looking up from the menu.

"I'm going for the grilled chicken sandwich and a salad. Hate to eat anything too heavy this close to bedtime."

Blake tossed his menu on the table. "Good idea. That sounds perfect. I'll get the same."

When Padraig returned with their beers, they placed their orders. Erika leaned back in the booth, lifting her feet to rest next to Blake on his bench seat. He grinned, reaching beneath her sock to tickle her ankle playfully, making her laugh.

For the next hour, he filled her in on the highlights of the game as they ate, going into so much detail, she felt like she'd been there.

She loved listening to Blake talk hockey. She hadn't been a fan of the sport prior to moving in across the hall from him. Her father's sports of choice had been the big three—football, basketball, and baseball. So that was what she'd been subjected to while growing up, forced to endure endless fall Sundays of him monopolizing the TV to watch his beloved Ravens.

Dad had also dragged her to countless Orioles games, the two of them attending at least three or four every summer for as long as she could remember.

The one sport her dad *hadn't* watched was hockey, so moving in across from Blake had opened her eyes to a whole new world in terms of sports. Not that she'd been an easy convert. Erika preferred rom com movies and reading mysteries to watching any sporting event, but that didn't stop Blake from trying to show her the error of her ways during those early days.

She had to admit, he'd worn her down, and she'd found herself tuning in to watch him play whenever she wasn't at work. And even when she did miss a game, she always watched either the replay or highlights reel the next day.

Erika never ceased to be amazed by his talent—his speed on the ice, his puck handling, even his incredible force when he checked someone into the glass. He was the most graceful brute she'd ever seen…and while she would never tell him, she understood why puck bunnies existed. There was nothing hotter than a guy on skates throwing a punch in defense of a teammate done wrong during the game.

"Poor Coulton is going to have a hell of a bruise on the side of his neck," Blake continued, describing a rather nasty hit the Rays' goalie had taken in a pileup in front of the net. "He stopped them from scoring, but damn if he didn't get his bell rung."

"I thought the goalie's helmet covered practically everything."

"It's no protection when you've got your head turned, watching the puck, and some dumbass blindsides you because he's coming in too fast and hard. Tank taught the guy a lesson—which he should have—but it set Tampa up to score on the power play. Whole night was just one fucking dumpster fire," Blake grumbled, taking the last swig of his beer.

"You'll get them next time," she said, pulling from her repertoire of pep talks. She used to really try to console Blake after a loss, but time and experience had taught her there was nothing short of a good night's sleep that would end his brooding.

While Blake was down tonight, by morning, he'd be back to his optimistic, competitive self. It was probably one of the best things about him. He didn't dwell on bad things for long.

"What the hell?"

They both glanced up as Tank walked over to their table, taking in their mostly empty plates. He put his hands on his hips. "How long have you two been here?"

Blake was quick to lift his hand in surrender. "Erik and I just stopped in for a quick dinner because she was too busy in the ER to eat tonight. We were going to say good night to you guys on our way out."

"What's up, Doc?" Tank—the affable giant—asked, giving her a friendly smile along with his standard Bugs Bunny greeting. She'd hung out with Blake and his teammates quite a lot over the past few years, and somewhere along the line, she'd become a part of their gang, invited to all the happy hours, pizza nights, and the monthly video game competitions Tank hosted at his place.

"Same old, same old. Listening to this one grumble and groan about losing tonight," she joked, jerking her thumb in Blake's direction. "Trust me when I say I've been taking one for the team, entertaining him alone rather than crashing your party back there." She gestured toward the back of the pub, where Tank had been sitting.

"Damn, you're a good person to take that on, because he's the sorest loser on the planet," Tank said, piling on.

Blake snorted. "That's funny, because I'm pretty sure I wasn't the one who punched his locker tonight after the game."

Erika's gaze slid to Tank's hand, spotting his bruised knuckles, before raising her eyebrows in a "really?" expression.

Tank caught her staring and grimaced as he tried to hide the evidence by shoving his hands in his pockets. "I took one too many bad calls tonight, then I got in a fight."

Erika noticed the dark bruise on Tank's chin. "Blake told me."

He lifted a shoulder casually. "Losing was the last straw, so I sort of lost my shit in the end."

She laughed softly. "You two are birds of a feather."

"You should have joined us back there because it's a regular pity party. We're all in the same funk. Misery loves company and all that shit." Tank tilted his head toward the table of teammates and puck bunnies.

"Yeah, well, I was trying to avoid—"

Before Blake could complete his thought, Mindy walked over,

sliding into the booth next to him, wrapping her arm around his shoulder and squeeing loudly.

"Blake!" Mindy said. "You came!"

Tank shot Blake an apologetic grimace, obviously aware of exactly who his best friend had been avoiding. Once again, Erika wondered why he didn't want to see Mindy. Sure, he had those stupid hookup rules, but he really was down in the dumps and for all her faults, Mindy seemed very adept at making Blake happy…in bed.

"Just stopped in for dinner. We're actually about to head out," Blake said, clearly trying to move Mindy back out of the booth.

His use of the word *we* had Mindy glancing across the table at Erika.

"Oh. Hey, Eva." Mindy's tone was considerably less friendly than the one she'd used for Blake.

"Erika," Blake corrected, while she rolled her eyes when he chastised the other woman for getting it wrong. After all, he continually insisted on calling her Erik. The stupid nickname had driven her crazy at first, but—like hockey—damn if it hadn't grown on her.

Erika had long since stopped trying to tell Mindy her name. Originally, she thought the other woman just couldn't remember it, but now she was starting to wonder if she was calling her the wrong name on purpose.

"Oh, right," Mindy said. "Why don't you stick around and join us?" Mindy was leaning close to Blake. Two more inches to the right and she'd be in his lap. "Or if you want, we can head out together. I can help you forget all about tonight's game."

Blake shook his head. "No thanks. You know the deal." He looked like he was going to say more, then reconsidered. Instead, he raised his hand, waving to Padraig for the check, clearly ready to move on now that they'd been spotted.

Padraig brought the bill, taking away the dirty dishes, as Tank and Blake chatted for a few minutes about the game.

Mindy interjected several of her own thoughts. Obviously, she'd been there, and Erika wondered if she went to all the home games. Erika attended as many as she could, but she'd never run into Mindy there. Not that she would expect to. The Baltimore Arena seated something like sixteen thousand people.

Once they settled the tab, Blake managed to scoot Mindy out of the booth and, as a group, they walked back to where Coulton, two more teammates, and a couple other women still sat, to say goodbye. Like Mindy, another woman, Lara, sidled up to Blake, whispering something in his ear. Erika recognized her as another one of his "victory dance" women.

Blake gave her a shake of the head and a smile.

"Ready to go?" he asked her, and Erika nodded, both of them anxious to make a quick escape when it became obvious Mindy wasn't finished trying to score a sleepover with Blake. In the end, he simply walked away from her.

Erika wondered if—okay, she hoped—the bloom was finally off the Mindy rose. She was surprised the woman had lasted as long as she had, because Erika couldn't begin to understand what Mindy and Blake even talked about.

She did an internal eye roll at that thought.

They didn't talk. They fucked.

Blake stopped short just as they reached the exit.

"Damn," he muttered.

"There's the rain," she said, glancing upward. The storm that had been forecasted had arrived with a vengeance.

Erika jerked when a flash of lightning lit the sky, her heart suddenly beating faster. She hated storms.

Blake leaned toward her. "Want me to go get the car?"

She shook her head. "No. It's not that far. Let's just make a run for it." Neither of them had thought to carry an umbrella into the pub with them, even though they'd known it was calling for rain.

Taking off together, they dashed down the block in the direction of the car, diving in as Blake unlocked it.

"Shit." He pushed his drenched hair away from his face laughing.

"We're soaked." She wished she could share his humor. Especially when a loud growl of thunder rumbled right overhead. She fought hard to hide her fear. She *really* hated storms.

Starting the car, Blake blasted the heat as they drove back to their apartment building. They high-fived when he found a spot near the front door, something unheard of at this time of night when most of the residents were already in for the evening.

Blake reached behind him, feeling around on the floor until he pulled out an umbrella. It was pointless, considering they were already dripping wet, but she still waited until he crossed in front of the vehicle and opened the door, covering her to keep most of the rain off.

They quickly walked toward the entrance, Erika digging in her purse as they went, looking for her keys, in a hurry to get inside and safe. Pulling them out, she promptly dropped the key ring, thanks to her stupid trembling hands.

"Damn." Crouching, she retrieved them, her attention drawn to a box next to a trash can.

It moved.

"I think there's something in there." She prayed it wasn't a rat because she'd lose her shit for real if it was.

"What the hell? Is that...whimpering?" Blake stood closer, trying to keep them both covered with the umbrella while attempting to peak into the box. He finally gave up the effort as he knelt down, pulling the lid off the box.

Erika gasped when she spotted the tiny black-and-white puppy inside the soggy box. The little thing was shivering, its fur matted from the rain.

"Oh my God," she exclaimed as Blake handed her the umbrella so he could reach in to pick up the puppy. "Did someone dump that poor little thing out with the trash?"

Blake rose, the three of them huddled beneath the umbrella.

His expression was pure fury. "Looks like. Takes a special kind of asshole."

"Come on. Let's get him—or her—inside." Erika kept the umbrella over Blake and the puppy, forgetting to be upset by the storm. She swiped her keycard over the scanner, unlocking the front entrance. One of the primary reasons she chose to move into this building was its excellent security.

Another whimper captured her attention. The puppy didn't look like it was much more than a month old, and she was concerned about getting it inside where it was warm and dry.

They took the elevator to their floor, Blake leading the way to his apartment. He handed her the puppy once they were inside. "I'll grab some towels from the bathroom."

Erika cuddled the shaking puppy close to her chest, cooing to it in a comforting voice. "You're okay, you sweet baby. Don't you worry. We're going to take good care of you."

Blake returned with two large bath towels. Laying one out on the island in his kitchen, he took the dog back from her, placing it in the middle while using the other towel to gently dry the puppy.

"Wonder how old it is?" Blake pondered aloud. "Doesn't look like it was just born."

Erika agreed that it wasn't a newborn, as its eyes were open and now that it was dry, it was starting to move around on the towel. She carefully lifted it, peering underneath. "A girl."

Blake used his pointer finger to stroke the puppy's belly, the action provoking the first tail wag and a little yip. He chuckled, then walked over to his fridge. "Poor little thing is probably hungry. Think she's old enough for solid food?"

Erika pulled out her phone and did a quick Google search. "I don't know," she said after scanning a couple of articles. She found an emergency "milk" formula recipe that Blake made, as they decided to play it safe in case the puppy was too young for real food.

He offered the milk to the dog, who quickly devoured it.

Blake only gave her only a little, since neither of them was sure what the puppy should be consuming.

Erika didn't have a clue what breed the cute thing was. Most likely a whodunit, though she thought she detected a bit of terrier.

"I can't believe someone would toss a dog out like trash. Especially on a night like tonight," she murmured, furious at the thought. "What would have happened to her if we hadn't found her?"

Blake didn't answer because he didn't have to. There was a good chance the puppy would have died. The rain was a cold one, the temperature continuing to drop. Without any way to stay warm or dry, she likely would have frozen to death.

Folding the towel a couple of times, Blake picked up the puppy, wrapping her like a baby in a blanket. Erika smiled at the tiny thing nestled in Blake's muscular arms. The puppy wriggled a little bit before settling down and closing her eyes.

"So sweet." Erika softly stroked the puppy's head. "I always wanted a dog when I was little."

"Never got one?" Blake walked to the living room, where he sank down on the couch. Erika followed him, not wanting to be too far away from the puppy.

"No. My mom was attacked by a dog when she was a kid, so she was terrified of them. Big or little, it didn't matter. I begged for a puppy for the better part of my fourth-grade year. I even wrote a letter to Santa, asking for one, so of course, I was *sure* I was going to get one for Christmas."

Blake handed her the puppy, still wrapped in the towel. "I'm guessing Santa didn't come through."

She grinned as she cuddled the tiny bundle in her arms. "Depends on what you consider coming through. I got a fluffy stuffed dog. I tried to pretend it was real, even going so far as to walk Corky on a leash. But dragging a toy around just wasn't the same thing."

"Corky?"

Erika laughed. "I have no idea why that was my chosen dog name when I was a kid, but I always said if I ever got a dog, I would name it Corky."

"Why haven't you adopted a dog since moving into your own place?"

"Doesn't feel fair to any pet I might get. I mean, I live alone and work long hours."

Blake nodded. "I get that. I'd love to have a dog. In fact, I've always said the first thing I'm going to do when I retire from the game is adopt one. But like you…it's not something I can do on my own. Hell, I'm on the road forty-five, fifty nights out of the year, depending on playoffs. There's no way I can take care of a dog properly."

Erika sighed, staring down at the sweet puppy in her arms. The tiny thing was sleeping soundly, clearly exhausted from the trauma of being left out in the rain in a cardboard box.

"I'm off tomorrow," she said. "I'll take her to the vet, get her checked out, make sure she's okay."

Blake twisted toward Erika, resting his arm along the back of the couch, his hand near her shoulder, his head bent close as he watched the dog sleep. "She is a cutie."

Erika nodded, then shivered, suddenly recalling that while they'd dried off the dog, the two of them were sitting there in damp clothing.

"Here. Leave her with me and go change into something dry." Blake rose, tilting his head toward the door in response to her trembling. He reached for the dog, but she was reluctant to hand her over.

Blake chuckled as he took the puppy from her. "Change your clothes, Erik. I promise I'll give her right back the second you return."

She begrudgingly agreed, anxious to stay with the dog. She felt a bit like that fourth-grade girl again, like she'd gotten a redo on Christmas and finally had her puppy.

Dashing across the hall, she quickly changed into a pair of leggings and a warm sweatshirt before returning to Blake's.

"Blake?"

"Back here."

She followed the sound of his voice to his bedroom without hesitation.

The two of them had quickly passed through the levels of association. Their initial interactions, after she'd put the kibosh on his flirting, had been that of just neighbors, but they evolved to friends swiftly, and best friends even faster, something that still amazed her to this day, as Erika had never found it particularly easy to make friends. She was too much of a bookworm, the type of person who spent a lot of time inside her own head. While she'd had people in her life she'd referred to as friends, when compared to Blake, she realized she'd be better off referring to them as acquaintances.

None of those other relationships came close to what she shared with him.

Erika hadn't lived here more than five months before she and Blake had swapped apartment keys. Somewhere along the line, their refrigerators had become shared property, he'd helped her paint her living room, and she'd basically redecorated his entire apartment, proclaiming he was a professional athlete, not a damn frat boy, and that he needed to live like the former.

The only line they'd never crossed was from friends to lovers. Blake was determined to hold on to his bachelor status, and while she wasn't actively dating at the moment, she knew she wouldn't be happy in a casual relationship. When it came to romance, she considered herself an all-in girl.

She'd mentioned her recent loneliness to Blake, but it was the one area where he couldn't understand or relate. Erika had brushed it off as a temporary funk. But the truth was, the feeling had been there for months…and it was growing.

Not the type to let things fester, she'd finally decided it was time to take action. So last week, just after admitting her loneliness to Blake, she did the one thing she'd always sworn she wouldn't do—she'd researched the best apps for those who weren't just looking for a hookup and uploaded profiles to eHarmony and Zoosk.

With any luck, she'd meet someone interested in a serious relationship and—please God—marriage and kids down the line. She was nearing the end of her last year of residency, so she was finally in a place where she felt like she had time to commit to dating.

Blake was pulling a T-shirt on as she entered, and while she shouldn't ogle her best friend, that was easier said than done. The man had a serious six-pack, the kind of rock-hard abs most guys would kill for but very few possessed.

His teammates had all remarked at one time or another about her and Blake's relationship, suspicious that it was more than they were letting on. For some reason, it was difficult for them to believe that a man and a woman as close as the two of them could be just friends.

Blake gestured toward the bed, where he'd placed the puppy. "She's all yours."

Erika stepped around the bed, fully intending to pick the dog up...but she couldn't do it. The poor little thing was snoring softly, obviously warm and comfortable after God only knew how long in that cold, wet box.

Rather than grab her, Erika sat down on the bed, reaching out to stroke the tiny dog's head.

Blake claimed the other side, resting his large hand on the puppy's body. "She's so small."

"And so adorable," Erika added. "I can't stop looking at her."

It was getting late, but despite working a long shift, she couldn't make herself leave the dog. And there was something about Blake's demeanor that said he didn't want to give her up either.

"You're going to hog her for the night, aren't you?" she murmured.

Blake gave her a grin, raising one eyebrow, that screamed "What do you think?"

She sighed, then shifted until she was lying down on the edge of the bed. "I'll just stay a little longer."

Blake chuckled, the sound calling her out on her lie, then followed suit, lying down as well, the two of them flanking the dog, facing each other.

"So what happens after the vet?" Blake asked, his eyes locked on the sleeping dog.

"I…" Erika knew what she should say. She should say she'd drop her off at a shelter…but even as she thought it, she knew there was no way in hell she would do that. The puppy had just been imprisoned in a box. How on earth could she do something that would put her back in a cage? "I don't know. I guess we could hang signs in the building. See if anyone would be interested in adopting her." Erika hated that idea as much as the shelter one.

"Yeah." Blake sounded just as unenthusiastic.

They kept petting the little dog, who opened her eyes briefly, giving them a giant, endearing yawn.

"Go back to sleep, Corky," Blake whispered.

Oh shit.

He'd given the puppy her dog name.

Just like that, Blake had sealed her fate…and the dog's.

Erika's gaze flew to his, perfectly aware her best friend's thoughts were traveling along the same path as her own. Blake wasn't giving this dog up any more than she was.

"We can't take care of a dog on our own…but that doesn't mean we couldn't take care of one together," he said.

Even as he said it, Erika could think of a million and twelve reasons why his suggestion was a bad idea. But she dismissed every single one.

"What about when I work nights and you're on the road?" Erika, sensible to a fault, thought she should at least offer a token amount of resistance.

Blake considered her question, then grinned. "Ashley."

Erika laughed quietly. Fifteen-year-old Ashley lived on the floor below them and had built a babysitting empire within their apartment building. Blake swore the girl was going to earn her first million before graduating from high school.

"She could walk Corky, feed and play with her on evenings when we're not home," Blake continued.

Erika nodded as an organizational schematic—one of her favorite things in the world—started to take shape in her mind. "We can print out monthly calendars with our work schedules, figure out who gets her on what days, when we'll need to hire Ashley."

She'd get online first thing in the morning to find cute whiteboards for their apartments. No, she quickly reconsidered, recalling a digital organizer she'd seen once with a touchscreen. She would get them each one of those.

Blake smirked. "You're already organizing everything in your head, aren't you?"

She nodded. "You know I love schedules."

"And yet you can't remember to feed yourself," he murmured. "You're an enigma, Erik." Then he grinned widely as he bent down to place a kiss on the puppy's head. "We can do this."

"This is insane," she whispered, not bothering to mask her excitement that they were keeping this puppy.

"No, it's not. It'll be great." There wasn't a hint of doubt in Blake's tone.

Erika lived alone by choice, after two crappy roommate experiences. As soon as she'd gotten to a place financially where she could live alone, she'd done so. And while she liked having a place all to herself, it would be nice to have some companionship to help ward off the loneliness that had taken residence. She still intended to date, but damn if the idea of having a dog to snuggle with at night while she found her Prince Charming didn't hold a lot of appeal.

She used the tip of her finger to run it down the puppy's nose. "I can't believe we're doing this." Then, because it was her and she was nothing if not a planner, she started running down her mental list for Blake. "After the vet tomorrow, we need to go shopping. We'll need food and water bowls for each of our places, and dog beds. Leashes and a collar. We can get a tag with both of our phone numbers on it. We need to research the best ways to train a puppy too. I know there's a crate-training method that we—"

Blake's scoff threw her off, then she narrowed her eyes.

"We need to train her," Erika insisted.

He simply held her gaze without replying.

"Shit. You're going to spoil her rotten, aren't you?" she asked.

He grinned. "I think we both know the answer to that question."

"Blake," she started.

"When Corky is with me, she's sleeping in my bed," Blake said. "We're going to cuddle."

She was already aware there was no way Corky wasn't sleeping with her too. God. She was already dreading the nights when Blake got her, and she didn't.

"I think the idea of crate training is for when you're not home," she pointed out.

He continued to shake his head. "I'm not shutting her in some damn box, period. It might traumatize her after what she went through tonight."

When he put it that way, Erika had no way to argue back. "I guess we could go the paper-training route." Then she added, "I'm ridiculously excited about this."

"So am I. But…"

"But?" she prodded.

"I think we're about to have our first puppy fight."

Erika frowned. "Already?"

"Yep." Blake glanced down at Corky. "Where is she sleeping tonight?"

Damn. He was right.

"Flip a coin?" she suggested, wondering if she could convince him to go best two out of three if she lost the first toss.

Blake shook his head, rising and leaving the room. Erika didn't bother to call out after him, cuddling with Corky instead.

When Blake returned, she realized he'd turned off all the lights in his living room. Grabbing a blanket from the top shelf of his closet, he switched off the bedroom light, the streetlamps and moon shining through the window allowing her to watch as he returned to the bed.

"Crawl under the covers, Erik," he said as he resumed the spot he'd just left, shaking out the blanket and throwing it over himself.

She didn't bother to argue, climbing under the duvet carefully, trying not to disturb Corky, who was happily sacked out between them.

"Good night," Blake murmured, his hand brushing hers as they both reached out to pet Corky.

"Good night," she whispered, closing her eyes, that feeling of loneliness, which never seemed to leave her alone, fading for the first time in a very long time.

CHAPTER THREE

BLAKE WAS on the way to his apartment, but he stopped midway between his place and Erika's when he heard her raised voice.

"Corky! What the hell?"

He grinned, quickly changing direction.

They'd just finished their first month of co-parenting a puppy, and the last four weeks had not been without challenges. Despite her early trauma, Corky had rallied quickly, going from a timid, shivering pup to a spoiled diva within a matter of days.

Blake thought they had turned the corner on potty training, so he hoped Erika's current distress wasn't because of yet another accident.

Their initial visit to the vet confirmed that Corky had been around six weeks old the night they'd found her. Given the storm she'd been dumped in, the vet said the fact she'd been a bit older and not a newborn had most likely saved her life. As far as breed, the best they could tell was Corky had a bit of Jack Russell Terrier and Chihuahua in her. The rest was a mystery.

She was still small, and as adorable as she'd been the night they'd found her. Blake was one hundred percent in love with the tiny creature, and despite Erika's harried tone right now, she was just as smitten. They were neck in neck when it came to spoiling Corky, and he wasn't sure who had more dog toys in their apartments currently.

He'd given Erika shit, claiming she'd gone off the deep end when she'd bought Corky a Halloween costume, but there was no denying the dog looked cute as hell as Winnie the Pooh. And while he'd pretended Erika had gone too far, it was hard to defend that argument, given the fact Corky in her costume was currently the picture on the home screen of his phone.

He did his standard one knock on her door, entering before Erika called out, "It's open."

It was her night to keep Corky, but she'd left the door unlocked as usual, aware he would want a quick snuggle after the game.

Blake smiled as Corky sprinted toward him, her tail wagging a million miles an hour as she yapped her happy hellos. He bent over to pick her up, laughing as she plastered his face with her sweet doggie kisses.

Erika looked decidedly *less* happy to see him.

"Everything okay?"

She held up a destroyed shoe. While they'd made their way through the potty-training stage, the teething stage was kicking off in grand style. Blake was going to have to replace one of the chairs in his living room, as Corky had done a number on two of the legs.

"I forgot to close the closet door," Erika said with a sigh. "I wasn't paying attention and it didn't occur to me until too late that she'd been quiet for too long."

He gave her a sympathetic grin. "Nothing worse than a silent Corky."

"Yeah." Erika turned away from him, and it occurred to him that she hadn't actually looked at him since he'd walked in. What he'd originally thought was annoyance looked more like sadness as he took in her slumped shoulders.

Blake closed the apartment door, setting Corky down. She

immediately scampered over to the couch, hopping up to settle down on her special blanket. Neither he nor Erika made any attempt to keep their baby off the furniture, both letting her sleep in their beds when it was their night to keep her, just as they'd said they would.

Erika grabbed her empty wine glass and walked toward the kitchen. "How was the game?"

"We won." He followed her, curious about her demeanor and her unwillingness to look him in the eye. "You didn't watch?"

She shook her head. "Did you score?"

"Yep," he replied, even though he didn't really want to talk about the game.

That response seemed to trip her up, as she paused for a moment, frowning. "Then why are you here? Shouldn't you be taking a victory lap with Mindy."

Mindy had certainly thought so, texting him about five seconds after the final buzzer.

Blake had finally done what he should have done a month ago, telling her their arrangement was over. He simply wasn't interested in her anymore. It had been fun and games and good orgasms for a while, but her sudden clinginess had opened his eyes to all the things Erika had been pointing out for months— like the woman's high-pitched, grating giggle, her flightiness, her lack of drive or ambition. Mindy had worked at least half a dozen different jobs in the year he'd known her and been unemployed for the last month, claiming she couldn't find anything that was the "right fit."

His teammate Victor—the grumpiest fucker on the planet— was convinced Mindy was hoping Blake would put a ring on it, so she could spend the rest of her life as a trophy wife.

"I called it quits with Mindy."

"Really?"

"Yep," he said.

"And how did she take that?" Erika asked.

Blake sighed. "Truthfully, I'm not sure she believes I'm serious." He'd expected some kickback from her, but all he got was a breezy promise to see him soon, as if he hadn't just told her that he didn't want to continue their affair. Which meant, he was going to have to go through the process of brushing her off again. Maybe he would just block her number instead.

Erika gave him a quick glance over her shoulder before turning back toward the fridge. "Water?" she offered. "Or wine?"

"Water, please."

"I didn't think you and Mindy were an official item, something that you needed to actually call off." She pulled out a bottle of water, then grabbed an almost-empty wine bottle, pouring what was left into her glass.

"We weren't, but she was starting to see a different future for the two of us, one I'm not interested in."

Erika's eyes were downcast as she put the bottle of water on the kitchen counter in front of him. However, now that he was closer, he could see her face—and he understood why she'd been avoiding his gaze.

He reached across the counter, gripping her chin, tilting her head upward. Her eyes were red and slightly puffy. "Have you been crying?"

Blake had known Erika nearly three years, and he'd *never* seen her cry. Not once. Given the things she saw on a day-to-day basis during her tenure in the ER, he figured she had a reason to fall apart at least once a week, but she never did.

"No," she lied, twisting her head to break his grip. "Allergies."

"Liar. It's not allergy season. You've been crying."

She walked around the island, out of the kitchen, and back to the living room, setting her wine glass on the coffee table. "I'm fine, Blake. I'm just tired. In fact, I think I'm going to call it a night."

It was an obvious attempt at dismissing him, and also a lie, considering she'd just refilled her glass. If she wasn't so upset, she wouldn't have even bothered trying to get rid of him because she knew as well as anyone that he was like a dog with a bone when he wanted to know something.

Rather than take her hint, he put his water next to her wine, then reached for her hand, pulling her down next to him on the couch. Corky lifted her head from her end, her sleepy eyes blinking at them a few times before she shifted positions and went back to sleep.

"Blake." Erika attempted to stand again, but he wrapped his arm around her shoulders, keeping her down.

"What happened?"

She resisted his grip for a few seconds more before relenting. "Just a bad night."

"At work?"

She nodded then—finally—met his gaze. "I'm fine," she repeated again.

"You trying to convince me or you?"

She pursed her lips.

Blake raised one eyebrow, letting her know without words that he knew he'd hit the nail on the head. "Talk to me, Erik."

"I don't want to bring you down. You won. You should be celebrating."

He scoffed. "I don't need to celebrate every damn win."

She rolled her eyes, a half-hearted attempt at playfulness. "Since when?"

"What happened at work?"

"I lost a patient," she said, her voice suddenly growing thick.

He gave her a moment to compose herself, wondering what set this patient apart from others she'd lost. Erika was a compassionate person and a dedicated doctor. Losing patients always affected her, but he'd never seen her fall apart like this. Her strength amazed him, so he hated seeing her so down.

"I'm sorry," he murmured when she failed to say more.

"Her name was Sara. She was seventeen."

"Fuck," Blake muttered. "That's rough. Car accident?"

Erika shook her head. "OD."

He wasn't sure how to respond to that. Sadly, Baltimore had been dubbed the U.S. Heroin Capital in a recent news program, so Erika had dealt with too many overdoses in her career.

"Heroin?"

"No," she said. "Cocaine, actually. She and her boyfriend got their hands on some bad stuff, laced with fentanyl."

"Fucking drugs."

"Her parents didn't even know she wasn't home in her own bed."

"Jesus," Blake whispered.

"She was an only child."

Ah. Maybe that explained it. Erika—also an only child—must have felt some sort of personal connection to the family.

"The worst part of my job is telling people they lost someone they loved. But when it's someone so young and it's unexpected and…"

Blake reached for her hand, squeezing it gently.

"There's nothing harder than watching parents come to grips with the fact they lost a child. Sara's father just stood there after I told them she was gone. Still as a statue. I've never seen anyone so devoid of…*anything*. It was like the light inside him went out completely. And Sara's mother didn't seem able to process what I'd said. She just started talking, really fast, telling me about her daughter's new boyfriend, about how they didn't approve of him, and how they'd grounded her for sneaking out to see him a few nights ago. Then she told me that her daughter was a good girl, always on the honor roll. Apparently, Sara had gotten early admission acceptance to her first choice of college. She wanted to be a math teacher."

Blake realized it wasn't just the mother who felt the need to talk. Now that she'd opened up, everything that had been bothering her fell out of Erika. He noticed there were no more tears. He wondered if that meant she was all cried out or if she never allowed herself to cry in front of others. Knowing Erika, he tended to think it was the latter.

"It sounded like Sara met the wrong boy, made a bad decision. One bad decision and then…nothing." Erika bent forward, reaching for her wine glass, then putting it right back down again without taking a drink.

"Did you open that bottle tonight?"

The sideways glance she gave him answered the question without words. She took a couple of deep breaths, and he watched her dig deep for that inner strength, shrugging off the heavy feelings. "I'm usually better at leaving stuff like this at work. This one…followed me home."

He knew what she said was true. "Is the wine helping?"

She shrugged, so Blake reached out, massaging her shoulders.

"You're damn tense for someone who's three glasses deep. You need some stress relief."

She gave him a small grin, the first genuine one of the evening. "It's too late to go running."

"We could always hit the gym downstairs. Race each other on the treadmills."

She shook her head. "You just played hockey all night. I can't imagine you have enough energy to run with me."

Blake hated seeing her so down. If it took running five, even *ten* miles to help her forget her sadness, he'd do it. "I've got plenty of steam left."

"I'm not sure I should get on a treadmill tipsy," she said, pointing to her wine.

He hadn't considered that. "True. You'd probably fall off," he joked.

Erika tilted her head left, then right, stretching the tense muscles. "Unfortunately, I can't employ your tried and true."

"What's that?" Blake asked.

"Orgasms."

He snorted, shocked and amused by her words. While he

was the king of TMI when it came to discussing his sex life with his best friend, she never shared any insight into her own. Of course, Blake knew his penchant for oversharing came less from wanting to brag and more from wanting to make her blush. Erika's cheeks went adorably pink every time he said something she considered scandalous.

"Of course you can. In fact, that's an excellent idea," he said. "Sex is to tension what aloe is to burns. There's nothing like knocking one off in a hot shower to send all your worries right down the drain."

"Wow, that's deep," she joked. "Did you rip that right off the SAT test?"

Blake laughed, glad to see the sadness was slowly fading from her eyes, giving way to teasing. "I don't think I'm the first person to discover that sex is a great way to relax. That's exactly what you need tonight."

She narrowed her eyes. "I know you like to take your victory lap, but I'm not sleeping with you just because I had a bad night and you had a good one."

Blake rolled his eyes. "Jesus, Erik. Don't worry. I'm not offering. You don't need a man to come."

"Really?" she replied sarcastically.

"An orgasm would help," he persisted, tilting his head, pretending to study her face. "Actually, in your case, it might take two."

Erika shook her head. "I swear you have sex on the brain. You do realize it's not the answer to every problem, right?"

"Since when?" he asked, aghast. "All I'm saying is, if you combine that wine with a hearty dose of masturbation, you'd sleep like a baby."

"I'll take your suggestion under advisement."

Blake could tell from her tone she'd already dismissed the idea. While she'd mentioned orgasms as a joke, the more he thought about it, the more he was sure it would really help. Now that she was brushing him off, he felt the stubborn need to double down.

"I'm being serious. When was the last time you had an orgasm?"

"I'm not answering that question." Erika grabbed the wine, upended the glass, drinking down the last of it.

"Are you counting in days?" he continued. "Months? Years?"

Erika shook her head, taking an imaginary key and locking her lips. "I'd never give you that much ammunition to use against me for future teasing."

Blake leaned back on the couch, resting his arm on the cushion behind her. "What's your sex toy situation like?"

"Oh my God. You have issues."

Blake laughed when he realized she was blushing, enjoying the sight of the pink now tinging her cheeks. "Let me guess. It's sparse. You probably own a Magic Wand and…" He rubbed his chin. "God, please tell me you at least own a dildo?"

Erika crossed her arms but didn't bother to add anything to the conversation. Teasing each other about sex wasn't a new thing for them. In fact, it was one of his favorite ways of getting under her skin. Probably because he viewed it as payback. Erika had a great deal of fun at his expense, constantly teasing him about his playboy habits and Mindy.

"Here's how I imagine your masturbation routine goes down," he started, encouraged to go on by Erika's unamused grin. "You press a vibrator to your clit for five to ten seconds, shove it inside for a dozen or so thrusts, give yourself a luke-warm orgasm, then fall asleep. You probably don't even bother to build the scene with a hot fantasy, do you?"

Erika smirked. "I'm not discussing my fantasies *or* sex toys with you."

"Toys? Plural? Hot damn." He rose from the couch, heading toward her bedroom. "Show them to me."

"Have you lost your mind?" Erika quickly followed, trying to cut him off as he reached for her nightstand drawer.

If she'd put any real effort behind stopping him, he would have relented, but her grip was weak at best. Once he opened the drawer, he understood why.

It was empty except for some lip balm, a bottle of aspirin, some tissues, and a crossword puzzle book.

"Erik," he drawled, about to close the drawer…when he spotted something tucked in the back. Reaching in, he pulled out a three-pack of condoms. "Condoms?"

She crossed her arms defensively. "Just in case. It doesn't hurt to have them on hand."

"The box isn't even open."

She grimaced. "Truth be told, that box made the move with me."

His eyes widened as he flipped it over. Jesus. How long had she had these? "They expire in a few months."

She leaned forward, glancing at the expiry date. "Really? Damn. Guess I should replace them."

He wanted to say why bother because she obviously didn't need them. Instead, he tossed them back in the drawer and closed it. "Toys?" he prompted, expecting her to tell him to go take a flying leap.

What he did *not* anticipate was her sinking down to the edge of the mattress, bending forward, and reaching under the bed to pull out a shoebox.

Placing it next to her on the bed, she lifted the lid.

Blake sighed at her pathetic collection. "Seriously? One vibrator, lube…and where the hell did you find a dildo that small?"

She scowled. "That's not small. It's perfectly average."

Blake's definition of average and hers differed greatly. Then he realized she'd inadvertently given him some insight into her past lovers. "How often do you play with these?"

She glanced at the box, shrugging one shoulder. "Not very often. I haven't really mastered masturbation." Then she giggled at her choice of words, reminding him she'd drunk quite a bit of wine tonight.

He should probably grab her a bottle of water, a couple ibuprofen, and tuck her in for the night. Instead, he asked, "What's that mean?"

"It's too *hard*," she said, with an adorable pout.

Blake couldn't help it. He laughed. "No, it's not."

"I think too much. And there's too much work to do to actually get myself there."

He found that tidbit both curious and interesting. Sitting down next to her on the bed, he twisted to face her. "Set the scene for me. Tell me what you normally do. Maybe I can offer some advice."

She laughed, even as she shook her head. "Oh my God, I've clearly had too much wine because I swear I'm actually tempted to tell you."

"Are you drunk?"

Erika considered his question. "Not really. I'd say I'm closer to tipsy."

That response convinced him to keep going. If she was wasted, he'd end things here. But Erika was in command of her faculties—she wasn't slurring or stumbling, and her eyes were perfectly focused on him. The wine was simply encouraging her to let her guard down a bit, something she didn't do nearly enough. He liked talking to her like this…liked hearing her giggle, seeing her blush, liked knowing that when she answered his questions, she was telling him the truth.

"So do as I said. When you masturbate, what's your routine? Does it vary?"

"No," she said without hesitation. "It's pretty much always the same. I use the vibrator on my clit to get myself wet. Sometimes it works, sometimes it doesn't. That's why I have lube."

Blake bit his lower lip to keep himself from showing any emotion, which was harder than he would have imagined. Right now, his emotions were overflowing, fluctuating between shock over her admission, annoyance that a beautiful, intelligent woman couldn't get herself wet, mild amusement, curiosity, and outright horniness.

"Okay. So what, then?" he asked when she stopped talking.

"I can't come from just stimulating my clit, so that's when I use the dildo. The problem is, it's awkward to try to keep the vibrator on my clit while fucking myself as hard and fast as I like. Then my arm gets tired, and I have to switch hands, and it just throws me out of the moment." She peered at him briefly through her long lashes. "It takes me a while to get there, even during *sex*-sex, so a lot of times I wind up getting frustrated and just quitting."

Blake frowned. "Are you just thinking about what you're doing? No fantasies?"

"Oh," she said. "I have a fantasy I play out."

"Just one?"

She nodded.

Blake had never considered masturbation from a woman's perspective. He'd watched past lovers get themselves off, and they never seemed to have much trouble. He wasn't sure if it was Erika's lack of experience or her inhibitions getting in the way. She was a doctor, for God's sake. She knew how the female body worked…and yet she hadn't found a way to master her own orgasm.

"What's the fantasy?" he asked, leery to hear the answer.

"There's this faceless guy—"

"Faceless?" he interjected.

"Well, obviously he has a face, but it's not someone in particular, like a movie star or anyone I know."

Blake nodded in understanding, gesturing for her to continue.

"He's on top of me, and I pretend he's playing with my clit and fucking me. While he's doing it, he's whispering in my ear."

Finally, Blake thought. *Something interesting*. "Whispering what?"

Her cheeks moved past the pink stage straight into bright red.

"You a fan of dirty talk, Erik?"

Her shrug was as good as a yes. "God. I can't believe I just told you all that."

"We're best friends," he said to reassure her. "I like knowing your secrets, and you know I'd never tell anyone else."

"Yeah, but that doesn't mean you won't tease me," she grumbled.

Blake thought about that and realized he didn't want to poke fun at her for what she'd just shared. Mainly because it didn't feel funny to him. The fact that she'd hit her thirties without learning how to give herself mind-blowing orgasms felt more like a damn crime.

"I'm not going to tease you. I'm going to teach you."

She frowned. "I'm serious, Blake. I'm not having sex with you."

He narrowed his eyes. "Again, I'm not offering." Rising from the bed, he picked up her two toys, then pointed to her lounge pants. "Crawl under the covers and take off your pants and panties."

She scoffed. "Hell no!"

"That wasn't a request, Erik. *Do it*," he demanded, his tone dark and dangerous.

She'd confessed to being turned on by dirty talk, so he couldn't help but wonder what other hot buttons she might have.

She blinked in response to his command. Then—sweet Jesus —she pulled back the duvet and climbed into her bed.

Blake walked to her bathroom, taking a few deep breaths to calm himself down. He'd meant what he said. He wasn't going to have sex with his best friend. Glancing down at his rock-hard erection, he reiterated that point in his head several times, trying to convince his stubborn cock that it wasn't going to happen.

When it refused to return to the at-ease position, he adjusted his pants and hoped Erika didn't glance in a southerly direction.

Washing her toys, he returned to the room, moving around the bed, pleased when he noticed her pants and panties lying on the floor. "Shift to the middle."

Again, she obeyed. "What are you going to do?"

"Do you trust me?"

Her head was bobbing up and down instantly, her quick response warming him. Earning her trust felt like winning the Stanley Cup, which was why he really needed to tread lightly right now.

Climbing onto her bed, he remained above the covers as he stretched out next to her.

Her breathing instantly became shallow. "Blake," she whispered.

"It's okay, Erik. I'm not going to touch you. Just guide you through this."

Her brows were furrowed, but she didn't tell him to get the fuck out. The appearance of her nipples, poking through her T-shirt made him think she was more excited than nervous.

He handed her the vibrator. "Slip this under the covers. Push the tip against your clit the way you like. Put it on the lowest setting for now."

Erika's hand trembled slightly, but she took the toy, following his instructions.

The sound of the vibrator filled the room, accompanied by Erika's soft intake of breath as the toy initially touched her clit. He couldn't see what she was doing, but he could tell from her facial expressions and breathing how the vibrator was making her feel.

Blake leaned closer, his lips at her ear. "Does that feel good?"

"Yes," she breathed.

"Is it making you wet?"

She nodded again, her hips lifting slightly. Her knee, tucked beneath the duvet, bumped against his thigh, telling him her legs were parted.

"Show me," he murmured, his face so close, her hair tickled his cheek.

Erika frowned until he clarified.

"Dip one of your fingers inside that tight pussy of yours and show me how wet you are."

Her gaze flew to his, and he thought he saw the slightest glimmer of panic.

"Close your eyes," he demanded. "And keep them closed."

She gave him one last look, and he held his breath, waiting for her to ask him to leave. His heart nearly exploded when she turned her head away, her eyes drifting shut.

"Now. Show me," he repeated, reminding her of his initial request.

Movement under the duvet told him she was doing as he asked, and a second later, one of her hands appeared from beneath the covers, her pointer finger wet with her own arousal.

"Such a dirty girl," he purred, watching her closely to see how she responded to his words.

Erika bit her lower lip, a soft whimper escaping.

Jesus. She liked it.

He forced himself to shut down his own needs and desires, fighting to disregard how in line their kinks seemed to be. He would never call Erika a slut or a whore, but he sure as shit liked calling her his dirty girl.

"Nice and wet," Blake praised, grabbing the dildo and placing it in the hand she still had raised for his inspection. "Increase the speed on the vibrator and slowly slide the dildo inside you. Don't fuck yourself with it. Just push it in to the hilt and hold it there." Blake made a mental note to buy her a proper fucking dildo. A wicked grin he was grateful she couldn't see tipped his lips upward as he decided right then and there to gift wrap one to slide under her Christmas tree.

More shifting of the duvet confirmed Erika was following his commands. He heard when the vibrator speed was increased and felt her hips lift off the mattress as she tried to slip the dildo inside.

Her breathing was labored.

"Is it inside you?"

She nodded. "Yes."

"Do you like having your tight pussy stuffed full of cock, dirty girl?"

Erika trembled. "God, yes!"

"How close are you to coming?"

The slight crease between her eyes told him there was still work to be done. Erika had admitted her orgasms took some work. Work she didn't seem to think was worth the effort. He intended to show her the error of her ways tonight.

"I—" she started.

"Shh," he whispered in her ear. "Close your legs around that dildo but keep the vibrator on your clit. Then shift your hips up and down."

Erika did as he said, her mouth falling open as she attempted to suck in some much-needed air.

"You're not going to come until I tell you to." Blake knew she wasn't close, but given her submissive responses to his demands, he suspected having her option to come stripped away would worm its way into her psyche, working against her. People want what they can't have.

"I—" she started again.

"I didn't give you permission to speak," he said, his voice louder after all his whispered demands. She jerked slightly in surprise, but damn if his tone didn't have the desired effect. Her hips started moving faster as the sexiest whimpers he'd ever heard fell from her lips. "Open those sexy legs, dirty girl. Spread them wide open and fuck yourself with that dildo."

His cock was harder than it had ever been in his life, and he didn't even want to think about the case of blue balls he was facing. Regardless, there wasn't a damn thing—short of a meteor striking the planet—that could make him stop. Watching Erika pleasure herself had pushed its way to the top five most beautiful things he'd ever seen in his life.

"God," she whispered. "Please!"

Blake was curious about her plea, then he recalled her comment that she could never fuck herself with the dildo as hard as she needed. He knew what he wanted to do...but it was crossing a line.

Erika groaned, and this time he heard the frustration behind it. She couldn't get herself where she wanted to be. He'd intended for tonight to be a lesson in masturbation, but that was wrong. The entire reason they'd started this whole thing was because Erika had been crying and tense.

She needed to come.

Blake clenched his jaw as he slid his hand beneath the duvet. Erika jerked when he brushed her hand away from the dildo. Her eyes opened briefly, but he shook his head.

"Close them. Let me give you what you need." He gripped the base of the dildo, the toy slippery from her arousal. He refused to let himself think about how easy it would be for him to pull down his pants and slide inside her.

Her pussy was so hot, he was surprised steam wasn't rising.

"Turn the vibrator on high and keep it pressed to your clit."

She did as he said—and then, he gave her exactly what she needed, pounding the toy inside her with a strength and force that had her hips rising from the mattress, a quiet keening cry of pleasure falling from her lips.

"Ohmigod!" she gasped, her body rising and falling in time with his thrusts, seeking and stealing as much as she could.

Twice, he felt the vibrator slip away from her clit, and both times, he snapped at her to hold it in place. "Let that thing fall again, and I'll flip you over and spank your ass."

Erika's groan, her full-body shudder, let him know just how much she liked that idea.

"You want to be a bad girl, don't you," he murmured in her ear. "A dirty, bad girl."

She nodded, just a single bob of her head.

"Tell me. Tell me you're a dirty girl."

Her lips parted, and he could see her struggle with the words. He slowed his thrusts, making it clear she wasn't going to get what *she* wanted until *he* did.

"I'm a dirty girl," she said softly.

Blake rewarded her by fucking her hard once more. He could tell by her cries she was getting close. "You want to come?"

"*Yes*," she hissed. "God, yes."

"Beg me."

Erika stuttered for a moment.

"Beg me, dirty girl. Beg me to let you come or—"

"Please," she cried before he could even finish making his threat. "God. Please. Please let me come!"

Blake pushed the dildo deeper as he gave her what she wanted. "Come," he demanded.

Erika's back arched off the bed as her lips parted, a silent scream erupting. Most of his lovers were very vocal in bed, downright loud even. Mindy was a screamer.

Erika was the exact opposite, her sounds so soft he almost couldn't hear them. Not that the volume mattered one iota. Erika's whimpers and cries, her quiet moans, were the hottest things he'd ever heard. Fucking music to his ears.

"That's it," he crooned. "Look at what a good girl you are."

Her orgasm started to fade, but Blake wasn't kidding earlier—one orgasm wasn't going to be enough. So he fucked her right through it.

Erika started to tremble, her eyelids fluttering.

"Don't you dare open those eyes. You're going to give me another one."

Erika was shaking her head, trying to deny him, even as her body responded to his rough fucking, to the relentless pounding of the dildo in her pussy.

"I can't," she gasped. "I never—"

"Take it," he demanded. "Take everything I give you, then scream my name."

That was all he had to say before her body proved her a liar, her second climax striking just as hard as the first, her body jerking like she'd touched a live wire.

"Fuck," she cried. "God. *Fuck*. Blake!"

Blake continued to thrust the toy inside her, but he moved it slower now, the motion intent on bringing her down easy. Erika went limp beside him, every drop of tension evaporated.

He pulled the dildo out, then reached over to turn off the vibrator she'd dropped during the second climax. She didn't react to any of his movements.

Her eyes remained shut, and for a moment, he wondered if she'd fallen asleep.

"Blake," she whispered, still not looking at him.

"Yeah," he murmured.

"Thank you."

He smiled, then pressed a kiss to her forehead. "Go to sleep, Erik."

She remained exactly where she was, not moving a muscle. Part of him suspected she couldn't. He'd fucked her boneless with the shittiest dildo ever made.

Rising slowly from the bed, he adjusted his pants, promising his dick he'd take care of it as soon as he got back to his place.

Corky must have heard him moving because she appeared in the doorway, looking as sleepy as her mommy. Bending over, he gave her a quick cuddle and head rub before placing the puppy on the bed next to Erika.

"Take care of our girl," he whispered to the little mutt before leaving her bedroom.

Blake took a moment to turn off the lights in her apartment, then locked the door behind him on the way out, aware he hadn't just crossed the line.

He'd fucking obliterated it.

CHAPTER FOUR

ERIKA ROLLED OVER AND GROANED, unable—or perhaps the better word was *unwilling*—to peel her eyes open. Her head hurt. Not that she was surprised.

That's what happens when you consume a bottle of wine.

Laying there, she let her thoughts play over everything that happened last night, her cheeks growing hot as she recalled not only showing Blake her sex toys but letting him use them on her.

Jesus. Christ.

She wanted to blame the wine, and in part, she did. It had certainly lowered her inhibitions because there was no way she would have engaged in a conversation about masturbation with Blake while sober. And there was no freaking *way* that discussion would have led them to her bedroom to do…what they did.

Holy. Shit.

She'd had what she considered decent orgasms in her life, but none of them held a candle to the two Blake had wrung out of her.

Two!

Erika was, and always had been, a one-and-done girl. Hell, most of the time, she was lucky if she got to one. She hadn't lied to her sexy neighbor when she'd told him that her orgasms took work, and some of her past lovers hadn't always expended that effort.

Of course, she shouldn't be surprised by Blake's mad skills. The guy liked sex, and he had enough of it that he *should* know what the hell he was doing in the bedroom.

Rubbing her brow wearily, she moaned, cursing herself.

What the fuck had she done?

They'd crossed one hell of a line last night, but even as she thought those words, she struggled to summon any actual regret.

Because…

Mother. Of. God.

It was the hottest sexual experience of her life. And Blake hadn't even removed a stitch of clothing. Hell, she hadn't even taken off her shirt and bra, she realized as she glanced down, now aware she was only naked from the waist down.

Erika forced herself to rise, throwing on the lounge pants she'd stripped off before crawling into bed. Tossing on some fuzzy socks, she made her way to the kitchen in search of water and aspirin.

Spotting the empty wine bottle on the counter, she blew out a long, slow breath.

It honestly felt like she'd had some sort of out-of-body experience last night because every single thing she'd done had been in direct opposition to how she usually handled things.

Usually, she was able to leave her work concerns at work.

Her wine consumption was limited to one or two glasses.

She didn't discuss her sex life.

Her willpower had never wavered when faced with Blake's undeniable sexiness.

She hadn't lost a lot of patients in her career, but she'd witnessed more than a few deaths. None of them had rattled her quite like Sara's. Not that she was surprised by that. Erika knew exactly why she'd let it get to her the way she had.

She'd seen herself in that young girl, recognized that fourteen years ago, it could have been *her* dying in that ER…all because of one very stupid, split-second decision.

Erika had looked at Sara's parents and seen her own. Imagined how they might have reacted if Erika's poor judgment had ended as tragically as Sara's.

She hadn't shared any of that with Blake because she wasn't that girl anymore. A single night had altered her trajectory, sent her down a much different path than the one she'd been traveling. And while she'd been young at the time, there was still a sense of shame—even after all these years—that kept her silent rather than confessing to Blake why Sara's death had shaken her so badly.

She'd appreciated his willingness to listen to her, and the compassion she'd seen in his eyes, the kindness, had comforted her. There was something about his presence that always steadied her and helped her find her footing. Perhaps it was because of his habit of taking care of her.

Erika considered herself an independent woman, one fully capable of handling her own shit…most of the time. She was assertive, confident, and comfortable in her own skin.

She didn't *need* anyone to look after her, but there was a difference between needing and wanting.

She made too many life and death decisions in her job, so many that she tended to shut down when she got home. She could diagnose and treat illnesses, rarely questioning what needed to be done to help her patients. But ask her what she wanted for dinner, and her brain went haywire.

When she moved in here, it hadn't taken Blake long to figure out she was a bit of a mess when it came to mealtimes, and the sweet man had taken it upon himself to help. As such, she received invitations to "friend" dinners two or three times a week, he helped her build her Instacart lists, and at least once a month, he dragged her kicking and screaming to the grocery store. And when she'd had to work overtime, more than once, he'd gone shopping *for* her, filling her fridge so she wouldn't have to worry about meals after her long shifts were over.

Erika knew she could do all of that herself—and if she had to, she would. After all, she'd made do prior to moving into this building.

But she *liked* how he took care of her, and she was touched by his concern.

So much so, it wasn't something she wanted to lose.

Which was why letting him use her sex toys on her was a stupid thing to do. How the hell was she supposed to face him now?

The dust hadn't even settled on that thought before Corky was racing to her front door, her tail wagging as she danced with glee. The puppy knew Blake's sounds, always warning Erika just before he arrived.

Sure enough, he pounded out one knock on the door before attempting to open it. She wasn't sure when they'd basically stopped knocking before entering. She wasn't even sure when they'd started unlocking their apartment doors first thing in the morning for each other.

All she knew was…she hadn't unlocked it this morning.

She couldn't.

Erika grimaced, flames licking her face. She wished she could act like the thirty-year-old woman she was and manage not to blush like a goddamn teenager in front of Blake.

Maybe it would be easier if he wasn't so ridiculously attractive. Erika wasn't going to deny that, upon first moving in, she'd thought long and hard about succumbing to Blake's overtures. He wore his jet-black hair slightly longer than most men she knew, though not long enough for a man bun or anything like that. Somehow, he managed to always have a five-o'clock shadow that showed off his chiseled jawline to perfection. And while he had a body that would make the archangels weep, the most stunning part of him was his piercing ice-blue eyes.

God, she could drown in those eyes.

Erika considered retreating to her bathroom and turning on the shower so Blake would think she'd hadn't heard his knock. It had taken her the first few months of living near him to stop drooling over his pretty face and lick-able muscles, but last night appeared to have undone all that hard work. Because now, as she stared at that closed door, all she could see was his heavy-lidded eyes watching as she came apart next to him…hear all those dirty, whispered words.

"Open the door, Erika," Blake demanded. "Or I'll use my key."

She groaned, perfectly aware he would follow through with the threat, especially considering he'd just used her full name.

Trudging to the door, she finger-combed her hair, attempting to tame it. She hated herself instantly for the effort because she'd stopped worrying about her appearance with Blake ages ago. They'd seen each other in all their facets—dressed up, dressed down, with bedhead, bedraggled by rain, and red-nosed due to allergies.

Erika unlocked the door, trying to hold Corky back with her foot so she could open the damn thing. Blake was prepared for the puppy when she finally managed, bending forward to scoop their beloved pet into one hand.

He grinned as Corky slathered him with a million licks.

Stepping in, he gave Erika a once-over that made her uncomfortable and horny all at the same time.

"None the worse for wear, I see," he joked, holding out his other hand.

"What's this?" she asked, accepting the smoothie, focusing her attention on the glass in order to avoid eye contact.

"My hangover cure. Drink it and I guarantee you'll feel better in half an hour."

She eyeballed the green smoothie. "What's in it?"

Blake chuckled. "Better that you don't know."

Erika stepped away from the door so he could walk in. She forced herself to turn back and head to the kitchen, planning to add a couple of ibuprofen to the smoothie cure. She also needed to stop looking at him, because while *she* probably resembled a scarecrow with her hair sticking out every which way, he'd taken the time to shower before coming over. He was wearing a basic button-down shirt and dark jeans. There shouldn't be a goddamn thing sexy about any of that, but for some reason, she found the entire ensemble ridiculously hot.

"How's your head?" he asked, following her.

"Crappy," she muttered, not looking him in the eye.

Blake stepped next to her, tapping under her chin twice. "Hey. Look at me."

She sighed, feigning annoyance. "I don't feel that great, Blake."

"I know that, but that's not why you won't look me in the eye, is it? Never known you to be a coward, Erik."

His words worked. She narrowed her eyes, glaring at him.

"There she is," he said with a grin that was too charming her for self-control.

"Blake—" she started, but he cut her off, shaking his head.

"You're not going to make what happened last night awkward between us."

She wanted to argue that fact because things were hella awkward at the moment.

"I mean it," he persisted. "We didn't do a damn thing wrong. Besides, it was a one-time deal. You had a bad night, and I tried to help."

There was no *try* about it. The man had succeeded…big-time. Not that she'd tell him that. One of her missions in life was to try to curb his cockiness.

"And I appreciate that," she forced herself to say when the silence drifted a bit too long. "It's just—"

"It's just nothing. Nothing has changed between us. We're still neighbors and best friends, co-parenting the cutest, sweetest dog on the planet. If you want to forget all about last night, that's fine. Or I'd be perfectly okay with you using the memory as your future spank-bank material because I think we can both admit, I rocked your world."

She rolled her eyes so hard, it hurt.

Blake laughed, then wrapped his arms around her, giving her a big, friendly hug. "We're okay, Erik. Okay?"

Every ounce of tension evaporated, thanks to that hug.

"We're okay."

"Good." Blake pulled away, walking to the basket where she kept Corky's leash. "I'm going to take our girl for a walk while you drink your smoothie. I've got practice in an hour. Might hit the pub afterward with the gang, so I could get back late."

She knew Blake's "gang" consisted of teammates and puck bunnies. The team had won last night, but Blake hadn't had a chance to celebrate, opting instead to cheer her up. Which meant, he would probably bring home one of his usual hookups for the night.

"You want to join us?" he asked, aware tonight was her night off, since her work and his game schedules were now emblazoned on digital organizers hanging in each of their kitchens.

She shook her head, lifting his smoothie. "No. I think alcohol and I are taking a break."

Blake ruffled her hair playfully, prompting her to smack his hand away. "Cool. You good with keeping Corky tonight?"

Yep, she decided. He was definitely hoping to get lucky.

"Sure," she said affably, hating that the idea of Blake bringing home a woman bothered her. That was something new and something very, very unwanted. Maybe they weren't as okay as she claimed.

Blake hooked the leash to Corky's collar, leading the dog to the door. Turning just before he left, he pointed to the smoothie. "Drink," he said in that deep, demanding tone that had pushed every hot button in her last night. "It'll make you feel better, dirty girl," he added with a shameless wink.

She flipped him the bird before lifting the glass, taking a big sip and grimacing at the taste.

He laughed loudly as he left, closing the door behind him.

Erika leaned over the counter, forcing herself to drink more of his hangover cure. Opening her phone, she checked her email and messages, finding one from Doug.

She'd met the financial analyst on eHarmony, and so far, they'd met for coffee twice. He was a nice guy, and while he wasn't Blake-level hot, he was certainly attractive. He'd messaged to invite her to dinner over the weekend.

Looked like she had passed the coffee-date hurdle.

She tried to decide if he had as well.

Yeah. She guessed he had. There hadn't been any apparent red flags, though spotting those hadn't proven to be one of her strengths, considering her past boyfriends. She shoved that thought away and she focused on Doug instead.

He was friendly and intelligent and a good listener. She hadn't really felt any sort of sexual attraction to him, but they also hadn't really tested those waters, both coffee dates ending with a simple handshake.

Erika glanced at the door Blake had just closed. He was going to go to that pub tonight, flirt with a woman, and then bring her home with him.

The loneliness she'd admitted feeling was still there. Blake obviously wasn't suffering the same because he was living the life he wanted. He didn't want a relationship, was more than fine with casual hookups, so that was what he indulged in.

Unlike her, he didn't let the grass grow under his feet, didn't let life pass him by while standing on the sidelines. How the hell did she expect to stop feeling lonely if she didn't put herself out there, didn't try to find the relationship she longed for?

She'd never been big on dating or partying, simply because she was always studying. Medical school, the boards, residency. It felt as if she'd spent ninety percent of her life with her nose in a book, preparing for the next test.

While she'd had a couple long-term boyfriends, both relationships had ended badly. So now she was left to wonder if she'd been using her schooling and her work as excuses to avoid the dating scene.

Fuck it.

No more excuses.

The time was right.

She was going to take a page from Blake's book and stop denying herself things that might make her happy.

Before she could think of an excuse not to, she replied to Doug's message, accepting his offer. His response came just a few minutes later, as he named a time and restaurant. She gave him a thumbs-up, then closed her phone, slowly sipping the rest of the smoothie.

By the time Blake returned with Corky, she was pleasantly surprised to realize her headache was gone, as was the queasiness in her stomach.

Once again, Blake had known just how to take care of her.

Only, right now, that didn't feel like such a great thing.

* * *

Erika toed off her shoes by the door, then slipped off Corky's leash. Walking to the kitchen, she poured herself a glass of iced tea, then headed to the couch, sinking down and propping her feet on the coffee table. Corky hopped up next to her, quickly settling in her lap.

She absentmindedly patted the dog's head. "Daddy will be home tonight, Cork." The dog wagged her tail, and Erika grinned, pretending Corky could understand her. Blake had been out of town, hitting the road for three nights of away games.

Talking to a dog might sound silly to some people, but considering Erika lived alone, it felt good to be able to fill some of the silence in the place with conversations. Even if they were one-sided.

Resting her head on the back of the couch, she sighed,

absently running her finger over her lower lip, recalling the good-night kisses she and Doug had just shared.

Two weeks had passed since his first invitation to dinner, and they'd gone out three times since, each time dragging out the goodbyes a little longer.

She knew Doug was waiting for the sleepover invitation, but so far, she hadn't issued it. She wasn't sure what was holding her back. Doug was great, and their dates had been fun. In addition to eating out, they texted occasionally, exchanging messages at least once every day or two. They didn't really talk about anything earth-shattering, just sharing little tidbits about their days, but it was still nice.

Tonight, they'd made out in his car outside her building like teenagers for a few minutes. Doug had rested his forehead against hers when they'd finally parted, clearly hoping she'd ask him in.

"I should have," she said aloud to Corky. "Why didn't I?"

Part of her knew. Actually, *all* of her knew. She just didn't want to admit it to herself.

While he was an attractive man and a decent kisser...she didn't feel any spark.

She'd had three lovers in the past. Just three. And while the sex had been okay, it sure as shit hadn't ruined her for other men. Now that she had Blake's masturbation lesson to use as a point of comparison, she didn't doubt for a second that sex with Doug wouldn't match up. It would probably be satisfying, and the ignorance-is-bliss Erika of old would have been perfectly happy with that.

This Erika?

She wanted her world rocked. Period.

Which was a problem she was going to have to overcome.

Because the more she got to know Doug, the more she suspected he was almost perfect for her in every other way. They shared the same interests, liked the same restaurants, laughed at each other's jokes, and had a good time together.

For someone who'd been bitching about being lonely, it felt as if Doug should be the answer to a prayer.

Personally, she blamed Blake for her current predicament. Because of the incredible orgasms and because she'd spent three years listening to the man talk about his sex life, drawing hot, kinky, horny pictures in her mind and building the act to a point that she couldn't make herself settle for less.

Dammit. The next time she and Doug went out, she was inviting him in, taking him to her bed and, if she had to, forcing a spark. For all she knew, he could be a sensational lover.

Corky, who'd been about to drift off, lifted her head from Erika's lap, looking toward the door. Erika didn't hear anything, but when Corky hopped off the couch and bounded over to the door, she knew Blake was home.

Erika rose as well, opening her door just in time to see Blake unlock his. Corky raced across the hall with a happy bark.

Blake turned around, bending down to pick up the dog. Erika couldn't help but notice the usual pep in his step seemed to be missing.

"Hey, Cork."

Yep, his tone was the definition of weary. When he looked at her, and she got her first good glimpse at his face, she understood why.

"Jesus, Blake!"

"Looks worse than it feels." He grabbed the duffel bag he'd dropped to grab Corky and walked into his apartment, leaving the door open for her.

She followed, closing the door then walking over to him.

Blake smirked, unsurprised when she crooked her finger, silently demanding that he bend down for her to check him out.

He had one hell of a shiner and a split lip that was red and puffy.

"Rough trip?"

He lifted one shoulder casually. "Won the first one, lost this afternoon's. Fucking Tampa had a hard-on for us, playing dirty as shit. Tank took a hard check into the boards, then three minutes later, the same fucking asshole high-sticked Victor, clipped him in the chin. I lost my shit."

Erika continued to examine him as he bitched, peering into his eyes to make sure they weren't dilated.

"You know the fight happened hours ago, and the team doc checked me out," he said, attempting to grin, then wincing when he pulled on the cut on his lip.

"Humor me."

"You didn't watch the game?"

She shook her head. "No, sorry. Missed it. I did catch the one a couple days ago."

Blake's eyes narrowed, and she wondered if he was pissed. She probably missed as many games as she saw, thanks to her work schedule, but it never seemed to bother him before.

"Are you wearing makeup?"

Erika frowned, confused by the question. "Yeah."

"Why?"

Now where the hell was *that* question coming from? It wasn't like she never wore makeup, though she usually didn't do more than swipe on some mascara and lip gloss. Tonight, she'd put in some effort prior to her date.

"I got back just a little while ago myself."

Blake crossed his arms. "From where?"

"A date."

She hadn't mentioned Doug to Blake. She wasn't sure why. That was yet another one of those annoying things that had been rolling around in the back of her head. Blake was her best friend in the world. And it wasn't like he tried to hide his hookups from *her*. They shared practically everything.

So, why had she hesitated telling him?

That same part that knew why she wasn't sleeping with Doug knew this answer too. But she refused to admit the reason, even if only inside her own brain.

"You had a date?" Blake's brows rose, like her going out on a date was the most preposterous thing he'd ever heard.

His reaction tweaked her temper because what was so unbelievable about her dating? She might not do it often, but it wasn't like she was undateable.

"Yes. I had a date."

Blake's surprise morphed to a scowl, and she decided she preferred his first response. "With who?"

"You don't know him."

"Is he another doctor at the hospital?"

She shook her head. "No. I met him on eHarmony."

"eHarmony?" Blake shouted. "What the hell are you doing on dating apps?"

"Oh, I don't know," she replied sarcastically. "Maybe looking for a date?"

Blake ran a hand through his hair, taking a step back.

Until he moved away, Erika didn't realize how closely they'd been standing to each other. He didn't reply immediately, and she got the sense he was taking a moment or two to calm down. Though she didn't understand his anger.

Or…maybe she did. Blake hadn't just assigned himself the caregiver role by reminding her to buy food and feeding her when she forgot to eat. He'd also assumed the job of her protector, always looking out for her whenever they were together. For instance, one night at the pub, a drunk guy had been hitting on her pretty hard. Blake had stepped in and sent the man packing. And that was just one example.

She hastened to reassure him that she wasn't doing anything stupid. "You don't have to worry. I met him at a busy coffee shop a couple of times, and the first time he invited me to dinner, I met him at the restaurant." Tonight was actually the first time she'd given Doug her address and allowed him to pick her up.

"What's his name?" he asked, still somewhat belligerently, if quieter.

"Doug." She withheld his last name on purpose.

He scoffed. "That's a pussy name."

She rolled her eyes. "No, it's not."

"What's he do for a living?"

Erika sighed heavily, letting him know she wasn't impressed by his fifth degree. "He's a financial analyst."

"Booooring," he singsonged.

She laughed. It was either that or slap her best friend. "He's very nice and interesting." Turning away from him in an attempt to stop the interrogation, she walked over to his freezer and pulled out an ice pack. Wrapping it in a towel, she returned, handing it to him. "You should put that on your lip. It's still swollen."

He started to do as she said, but froze, his gaze sliding to *her* lips. "Your lips are swollen too." Before she realized what he was doing, he reached out to caress the side of her mouth with his thumb. "Is that beard burn?"

She hated it, but she blushed, brushing his hand away. "Doug has a beard."

"So things are getting pretty hot and heavy between you two?"

She shrugged. "I don't know. Maybe."

"Hmph," he grumbled, grabbing his duffel and carrying it to his bedroom.

She followed. "You want Corky tonight?" She leaned on the doorframe as he upended the clothing in his duffel directly into the laundry hamper. "I took her out for her walk, so she's good for the night."

Blake didn't answer her question. Instead, he grabbed his toiletry bag and carried it to the bathroom.

She frowned. "You're being a grumpy ass."

"I'm sore and tired," he explained when he returned to the room.

"Okay. Then I guess I'll leave you alone." He hadn't answered her question about Corky, but she'd already decided to leave him the puppy. He'd been away three nights, and he missed their dog when he was away. Besides, maybe Corky could do a better job of cheering him up, since she was failing so spectacularly.

"You're going to leave? I'm hurt."

She crossed her arms. "I thought hockey players were supposed to be tough guys."

"I'm just saying, that's not much of a bedside manner, Doc. You'd leave a man to suffer?"

She wasn't sure how to respond because while his words felt like a joke, his tone was gruff and even a little bit hostile.

She raised one eyebrow. "Aren't you a ray of fucking sunshine tonight?"

For the first time, her words seemed to penetrate, cutting through his dark mood, provoking what she suspected would be a real smile if his lip wasn't hurt.

"I'm sorry. I'm a sore loser. You know that."

She did, and while she appreciated his apology, there was a tiny part inside of her that was disappointed to hear that was the reason for his grumpiness. She'd kind of hoped his moodiness had been driven by jealousy over Doug.

She needed to stop thinking that way.

He wasn't interested in her. He'd said so the morning after he'd blown her head off her shoulders with those two orgasms.

What had he called it?

A one-time deal.

Something he'd clearly meant because they'd gone back to the exact same friendship they'd enjoyed for three years. He hadn't flirted, hadn't touched her, hadn't given her any indication that he wanted anything more from her than they already shared.

She was the one who was letting her thoughts run rampant.

"Apology accepted," she said, walking over to him. "I'll leave you Corky. Cuddling her always makes you feel better."

He hmphed again, proving he still wasn't over his snit. Dropping down on the side of the bed, he glanced at her. "You're really going to leave me alone when I'm in pain?"

She laughed. "You have a cut lip and a black eye. I gave you ice. What else do you expect me to do?"

He pointed to his cheek, just below the ever-darkening bruise. "Kiss it and make it feel better."

Erika snorted. "I attended medical school for four years, and I'm in the fourth year of my residency. Trust me when I say nowhere in any of my medical books was a kiss the recommended treatment."

He didn't respond, just continued to point to his bruise.

"Fine. You big baby," she muttered, bending down to kiss his sore cheek.

Smirking, he tugged off his T-shirt, twisting so she could see the substantial bruise on his shoulder. He really had gone to war.

Rather than call him to task for fighting, she offered his shoulder the same "healing" kiss.

Blake, the shameless man, was now smiling, despite the pain it was probably causing him. She understood why when he pointed to his lip.

She tilted her head. "Seriously?"

"I seem to recall helping you out a few weeks ago when you were having a bad night."

It was the first time Blake had mentioned the masturbation lesson since the morning after.

"You did," she said quietly, the devil on her shoulder telling her to give him the kiss he was asking for, while the angel warned her she was flirting with disaster.

Her angel usually won the arguments, so she couldn't explain why she was bending forward once again.

She gave him a quick kiss, using all the willpower in her body to keep it as platonic and innocent as she could.

Unfortunately, she wasn't the problem. Blake was.

Because the second she started to pull away, he reached for her, gripping the nape of her neck, holding her in place while he stripped all the platonic out, replacing it with a kiss so passion-ate, Erika felt instantly light-headed.

She jerked when his tongue touched hers, but the shock didn't linger. How could it? Blake was kissing her senseless. Every reasonable thought fled as she slid her tongue out to meet his, her fingers gripping his thick hair, while Blake twisted her head so he could deepen the kiss.

Erika wasn't sure how long it lasted, but by the time she managed to regain her wits and pull away, she knew without a doubt they'd let it go on way too long.

She straightened, her gaze locked with Blake's. They were both breathing heavily after depriving themselves of air while they'd kissed like the plane was going down.

"We took that too far," she whispered, when the silence lingered.

She expected Blake to agree, but instead, he frowned.

"Blake," she said, desperate for him to say something. *Anything*.

"I'm a sore loser," he repeated.

She wasn't sure what to make of that…because it suddenly didn't feel like he was talking about the game anymore.

Especially when he added yet another apology—and a wicked grin that belied it. "Sorry, Erik."

His cocky smile and use of her nickname calmed her nerves about stepping over the line—again. Enough that she could walk away. "Good night, Balakay."

She locked his apartment door behind her, walking over to her own. Once she was inside, she leaned against her door, stroking her lips with the tips of her fingers, much like she had earlier on the couch.

She'd wished for a spark.

Well, she'd gotten one.

Unfortunately, it was with the wrong guy.

CHAPTER FIVE

BLAKE FLIPPED THROUGH THE CHANNELS, not landing on anything. He was too distracted. Three days had passed since he'd foolishly planted one on Erika, letting his damn jealousy get the better of him.

She'd gone on dates since moving in across the hall, so he wasn't sure what was different about this Doug tool. Maybe it was because that guy had somehow managed more than one date—or the fact she hadn't told him about *any* of them.

There were precious few secrets between him and Erika, so the idea that she'd hidden this guy—on purpose or not—bothered him. He liked knowing what was going on in her life, liked being her confidante, and he *hated* that she was dating some boring financial analyst named Doug.

Glancing over his shoulder, his gaze zeroed in on today's square in the digital organizer. The two wall-mounted screens were the first thing Erika had bought them after they'd decided to co-parent Corky. He had one in his kitchen, and the other was in hers. The things linked so whenever she added something to hers, it showed up on his.

She was nothing if not organized, the woman in possession of not one, not two, but *three* planners, as well as countless colored pens and a stack of stickers as long as his arm. She fucking loved organizers, so he shouldn't have been surprised when she outfitted them with the digital ones.

He had to admit they were pretty cool. The things were touchscreen, so it was easy to add and delete things as needed. Originally, the plan had been to simply use the shared organizers to post their work schedules so they would know who had Corky each night and when to plan ahead for nights when they'd need to hire Ashley to dog sit. However, he'd noticed that more and more information was being added to the organizers lately, including their day-to-day plans, like pizza nights with the gang, appointments, and—he sighed—apparently Erika's dates.

Yesterday, he'd awoken to see a new item written under today's date, proclaiming her dinner/movie plans with fucking Doug. It had already been his night to keep Corky, so he wasn't sure why she added it. Maybe it was because the woman seriously couldn't hold herself back when it came to writing things in her organizers.

Or maybe it was supposed to be a subtle message to *him*.

After all, Erika was the one who'd insisted from day one that the two of them should simply remain friends. And Blake hadn't had a problem going along with that…until lately.

During the past few weeks, he'd started blurring lines, like the kiss and the masturbation lesson, while giving into—*fuck*— feelings he shouldn't have for his best friend.

Blake blamed his prolonged bachelorhood on his job. He was on the road several nights a week, and when he'd first been drafted, he'd been too enamored with the countless puck bunnies lining up to warm his bed to consider settling down with one woman. Why eat cheeseburgers every night when there was steak and salmon and lasagna and a million other delicious things to sample?

But after ten years of dining from the all-you-can-eat buffet, he was hungry for something more, something meaningful.

There was such a thing as too many choices, and lately all Blake wanted was comfort food.

He snorted to himself, aware that Erika would read him the riot act if she heard him comparing women to food. And there was no way in hell she'd appreciate being thought of as comfort food, even if he did mean it as a compliment.

Leaning his head back against the couch, he sighed. He needed to shrug off these feelings that had started to develop for Erika. Blake refused to ruin a great friendship when it was abundantly clear he was the only one fighting this desperate need to cross the line they had no business crossing. He'd kept a lid on his physical attraction to her for years, so why was he suddenly so obsessed with her lips, her legs that went on forever, her smile, her hourglass figure?

While he'd jerked off three times the night of his "lesson," it hadn't helped at all—not then or since. Hadn't slaked his desire for more. For *her*.

Unfortunately, Erika hadn't looked at him in the same light the morning after. Shit. Until he'd forced her, she wouldn't look at him at all. And when she did, it was clear she was uncomfortable, not hot for more. Not that it should have surprised him.

There was no way Erika would have let it go as far as it had if she hadn't been tipsy and sad, so obviously in the sober, harsh light of day, she'd gone back to her analytical ways, falling back on all those reasons why they couldn't have sex.

And he'd let her. Desperate to put them back on firm foundation, swearing nothing had changed between them because he'd been worried she would push him away completely otherwise.

Mercifully, he'd talked her off the ledge that day…only to push her right back on it three nights ago when, in his grumpy asshole state, he'd pressed for a kiss "to make it better." The joke had been on him because that hotter-than-hell, not-the-slightest-bit-platonic kiss had made everything worse. A lot worse.

Erika was too good a friend to slap him or reject him

outright, so she'd gone the gentle route, quietly letting him know he'd taken it too far again.

Yeah, tell that to his dick.

Since then, he'd only seen Erika whenever they traded Corky, and during those times, she'd been perfectly friendly…but distant.

It was his fault he was suddenly looking at her and wanting more than friendship. His fault his cock had woken up and taken fucking notice of how gorgeous she was, with her shiny chestnut hair, her soulful dark brown eyes, and her smokin'-hot body. Erika had curves in all the right places.

"Fuck," he muttered, feeling Corky stir next to him at the sound of his voice in the quiet room. He'd muted the TV while channel surfing, only just now aware of how stifling the silence felt.

He reached over and patted the tiny dog's head, grinning when she licked his hand, her tail wagging, showing him how much she enjoyed his attention. "I keep fucking up with your mommy."

The fact she was out on a date with Doug should tell him in bright neon letters he was the only one wishing the status quo between them would change from friends to lovers.

Corky shoved her head under his hand when he forgot to keep petting her.

"Shameless girl," he said, chuckling. Corky had become quite adept at petting herself with his hand or, if she was laying on the floor, his foot.

Resuming his clicking, he finally stopped his search when he found a repeat of the old *Predator* movie. Turning off mute, he propped his feet on the coffee table and settled in to watch, repeating the words "get to the choppa" in his best Arnold impersonation. Not that Corky was impressed.

The two of them lay there for an hour before Corky's head suddenly rose from his lap, her attention turning toward the front door.

She was better than any security service Blake could buy when it came to letting him know Erika was home. The dog scampered off his lap, dashing for the door, waiting for it to open.

Blake held his breath for a moment, hoping she'd said goodbye to Doug on the street so she could stop in to see him and check on Corky.

When nothing happened, he sighed. If Erika was home and alone, she would have come by here before returning to her apartment.

Which meant…

He leaned forward, trying to talk himself into staying on the couch. The pep talk failed miserably as he rose and joined Corky at the door.

Peering through the peephole, he growled when he spotted Erika and Doug standing outside her closed door. The guy was giving her one hell of a good-night kiss.

Blake knew he should give them some privacy. A decent man would walk away and stop spying on them. Unfortunately, he wasn't decent. At this point, he wasn't even fucking nice. Because what he did was the opposite of the smart thing.

He opened the door, then feigned surprise when he spotted Doug and Erika, both of whom quickly stepped away from each other.

"Sorry," Blake said, as Corky sprinted across the hall, Erika bending to scoop the dog into her arms. "Thought Corky was whining because she needed to pee. Didn't realize you were home."

As far as lies, his was a whopper, and also a shitty one because it was instantly obvious to his intelligent neighbor that Corky wasn't wearing a leash for their nightly walk.

Doug was studying him with a curious expression, so Erika offered introductions.

"Doug Prescott, this is my neighbor, Blake Wright. Blake, this is Doug."

Doug glanced at Erika. "When you said you shared a dog with your neighbor Blake, I assumed you were talking about a woman." Then the man's gaze flew back to him. "Wait. Blake *Wright*?" Doug crossed the hall excitedly, his hand outstretched. "Holy shit! You're a center for the Stingrays! I'm a huge fan. Try to make it to as many home games as I can during the season."

Blake smiled, returning the man's handshake, pointedly ignoring Erika's narrowed eyes staring him down as if she was telepathically trying to tell him to fuck off.

"Nice to meet you," Blake said.

Doug launched into a conversation about the previous night's home game, which he'd apparently attended with some work colleagues. The two of them spent the next ten minutes rehashing the finer points of the game, which mercifully the Rays had won. Blake had even scored a goal, so it was easy for him to chat, secretly pleased that Doug was impressed by him. It soothed the ragged parts in Blake that were—*fuck him*—jealous that this man had gotten to take Erika out while he'd been hardcore relegated to the fucking friend zone.

Erika cleared her throat when the conversation carried on a bit too long.

"Oh damn. Sorry about that, Erika. I guess you busted me," Doug said good-naturedly. "I'm a bona fide, hardcore sport's fanatic. I usually try to hide that fact until at least the eighth date, lest I scare the woman away."

Erika giggled at the man's stupid joke. "I think I can deal with that. So long as your fandom doesn't involve painting your face or chest."

"No face paint." Doug crossed his finger over his heart, and Blake scowled, annoyed to think this guy was getting too fucking close to that eighth date. According to Erika, they'd had two coffee dates and four dinner dates, counting tonight. Turning back to Blake, Doug gave him a single nod of his head. "It was great to meet you, Blake."

"You too," Blake said, proud of how sincere his lie sounded.

Erika placed Corky down, the dog scurrying back to Blake as Doug returned to her. It was apparent this was the part where Blake was supposed to say good night and return to his apartment.

He wanted to do that.

He really did.

But it was obvious Doug was waiting for Erika to invite him in for a nightcap. Blake wasn't a hundred percent sure how he could stop that if she did, and he was a million percent sure he shouldn't try.

Reluctantly, he began to move back inside, pausing when Erika gave Doug the brush-off, claiming she was working the early shift at the hospital. Blake knew from the digital organizer that she didn't have to be at work until noon, and because he was him, he smirked to let her know he knew she was fibbing.

She shot him a dirty look that left him feeling less chastised and more amused as he called Corky's name, guiding her into his apartment to shut the door.

He hadn't made it three steps away from the door before it flew open. Blake twisted, grinning widely.

"What the hell was that?" She slammed the door behind her.

Blake frowned, pretending the question confused him. "What was what?"

"Why did you open your door?"

"I told you—" He started to repeat his lie, but Erika cut him off, rolling her eyes.

"Please. You didn't even have Corky's leash in your hand. You were spying on me."

He crossed his arms. "You can hardly call it spying when I was standing right where you could see me. I just wanted to meet the guy. See if he's good enough for you."

Erika placed her hands on her hips, and while he could see she was trying to be pissed, he didn't think she was as annoyed as she was acting. "Who I date is none of your business."

Blake shook his head. "Bullshit. You're my best friend, Erik.

You can be damn sure I'm going to check out your boyfriends to make sure you're not only safe but with someone who will treat you the way you deserve."

Erika tilted her head but didn't respond. He'd taken the wind out of her sails.

"Why didn't you invite him in?" He was curious if he'd changed the course of her evening or if she'd always intended to send the guy packing.

"I should have. I mean…I was thinking about it."

Blake frowned. "Thinking about it? The guy walked you all the way upstairs. Seems to me like you'd already decided."

She shook her head. "I hadn't." Then she glanced back at the closed door. "Oh my God. Do you think I was giving Doug mixed signals? He was the one who offered to walk me up. When he kissed me good night, I was trying to decide…" Her words faded away.

"You were trying to decide *while* he was kissing you?"

She shrugged. "I like him, and we have a good time together, but I'm just not sure I'm ready to take the next step."

Doug couldn't be much of a kisser if Erika was standing there making a list of pros and cons while the guy was laying one on her. He was tempted to tell her as much, but he knew her well enough to know that would really annoy her.

If he was a good friend, he'd convince her to invite Doug in the next time for a sleepover. The woman had gone too long between sexual encounters.

"When was the last time you had sex?"

Erika shook her head. "I'm not talking about sex with you again. We already had that conversation."

"More than two years? Three?" he guessed.

The way she stilled told him he was on the right track. "Why do you think that?"

"I live across the hall, Erik. Never, not once, have I seen any guy leaving your place in the morning…or in the middle of the night, for that matter.

"Just because I don't have a revolving door of lovers coming in and out of my place, doesn't mean I'm never getting laid." Her cheeks were flushed that adorable pink that told him she was lying though her teeth.

"My apartment is hardly a revolving door, if that's what you're insinuating." Blake headed to the kitchen, peering into his refrigerator. "Beer, wine, tea, coffee, or OJ?"

She followed him, leaning on the island counter. "Beer."

He popped the tops off two Coronas, handing her one.

"No lime?"

He chuckled. "Snob. I'll put them on the grocery list for next time."

They tapped their bottles together, not bothering to make a toast, each of them taking a long swig.

"So you like this guy?" Blake asked, not sure he wanted to know the answer.

"I guess so."

She was the queen of vague when it came to subjects she didn't want to discuss. Usually he let her get away with it, but not this time.

Blake took another quick sip. "You've gone out with him more than any other guy in the past few years. So I'm going to go out on a limb and say you like him."

"He's a nice guy."

Jesus. She was a professional when it came to being elusive. Not that it mattered. He knew exactly how to get her to talk. "It's a shame he's such a shitty kisser."

Erika frowned. "He's not a bad kisser."

He smirked. "Not bad doesn't not translate to great."

She put her beer down. "Doug's kisses are very nice."

"Nice is probably the most boring word in the dictionary. Don't mean to brag, but none of my lovers have ever called me or my kisses *nice*."

Erika rolled her eyes. "You realize what you just said was the very definition of bragging. And I'm pretty sure there's no way you can know they haven't said that about you."

Blake leaned against the kitchen counter, crossing his arms in a way that he knew made his muscles bulge. "Trust me. I know."

"You are the most arrogant, annoying, cocky—"

"Cocky and arrogant mean the same thing," he interjected.

"Thanks for all these vocabulary lessons, Balakay. You're in rare form tonight." She sighed. "But I'm too tired to play."

He hadn't noticed the dark circles under her eyes until she admitted to being tired. "You sleeping okay?"

"Yeah." He wasn't sure what it was about her tone or facial expressions, but he could tell she was lying. "You know what you need?" he asked as he spied a way to cheer her up…and keep her from going out with Doug this weekend.

Not that keeping her away from Doug was his primary objective.

Now who's lying? he thought to himself.

"If you say sex, I swear to God I'm going to walk out of this apartment and never come back."

He chuckled, then pretended to lock his lips and toss the key away on that subject. "What are you doing Saturday night?"

Erika, the clever woman, looked instantly suspicious. "Why?"

"Just answer the question," he pressed.

"I'm busy."

Blake laughed as he strolled over to the digital organizer, clicking on a button to show the weekend portion of the calendar. He already knew the answer to his question, noticing she had nothing listed under the date when he'd filled in his own plans.

"Hmm," he said, pointedly looking at the empty space.

"Fine. I'm not doing anything…yet. But there's a chance Doug might text me for a date."

Blake made a buzzer sound, indicating her answer was

wrong. "Nope. You're going to have to tell the not-bad-kissing nice guy that you're busy."

"Doing what?" Erika took a drink of beer.

"I have to go to this stupid charity event, some black-tie gala, and you're coming with me."

Erika responded by giving him back the same "wrong answer" buzzer sound. "Pass."

"Nope. No passes. You owe me one, and I'm collecting."

Her brows furrowed. "How do I owe you one?"

"I picked you up at work when your car was in the shop, and you said so."

She scoffed. "Those favors hardly match. You drove ten minutes out of your way to bring me home. You're asking for hours at some stuffy party with a bunch of people I don't know."

"You'll know plenty of people," he reassured her. "Tank, Coulton, Victor, Preston, and a few other guys will all be there with dates too."

"Take Mindy," she grumbled.

Blake shook his head. "Took her last year and…it didn't go well. One of the organizers of the fundraiser, an older gentleman and a widower, was there with his twenty-year-old daughter. Mindy made a comment about what a cute couple they were."

Erika giggled. "To be fair, Mindy's assessment of the male population probably falls into two categories, hot hockey players or sugar daddies."

Blake groaned because she'd hit the nail on the head. Mindy had made a remark after he'd explained her mistake to her at their table, asking if the widower was still single.

"I'm not taking Mindy."

"Fine. Pick another bunny."

He shook his head. "Nope. You're pretty and smart, you clean up good, you know the difference between the salad and dinner forks, plus, I don't have to worry about you embarrassing me."

Erika held up her hand. "Stop with the compliments. My head will explode."

Blake wiggled his eyebrows at her, chuckling.

She glanced back at the digital organizer. "Wait a minute. How long have you known about this event?"

Blake shrugged. "I don't know. A couple months? Maybe three?"

"You realize most women need longer than three days' notice for swanky parties. What makes you think I have anything suitable to wear?"

"Don't women have dresses for all kinds of shit?"

She sighed. "That's beside the point. You can't ask someone to something like this on the spur of the moment."

Blake gave her shit-eating grin. "All I heard was beside the point. Which means you have a dress."

Erika rubbed her brow, and for a second, he started to worry about her "tired" comment. She'd pulled a couple of late nights this week, covering for a doctor who'd been involved in a skiing accident and broken his ankle, so maybe she was feeling overworked.

However…this felt like a different kind of tired.

He hated the fact she was fighting him so hard because it drove home what he already knew. Erika didn't want to sleep with him.

If he wasn't such a cocky, annoying, arrogant man, maybe he could accept that with good grace. But he couldn't deal with the idea that fucking boring-ass Doug had gotten two coffee dates and four dinner dates, and he couldn't even convince her to go to a shitty charity event with him as a favor.

The entire idea of her picking Doug over him rubbed Blake wrong. So he embraced his new bad habit of doing something he shouldn't. Lucky for him, it was something he was also good at.

Seduction.

"Tell you what," he said, circling the island until he stood next to her. "Why don't you mull it over? I'll even help you. You think best when you're kissing, right?"

Before she could respond, he reached out, gripping her shoulders and pulling her close. His mouth was on hers in a second and he pushed her lips apart, his tongue dipping inside, tasting the beer. Her mouth was cold from the drink, so he worked hard to heat it, his breath mingling with hers, growing warmer.

Blake nipped her lower lip, then started exploring her mouth with his tongue again, making damn sure Erika was so focused on his kiss, her brain wouldn't have time to make a pros and cons list like the one she'd been composing for Doug.

He half expected her to push him away, like she had the other night in his bedroom, so he went for a tighter grip. He released her shoulders, moving one hand to the nape of her neck to hold her in place, the other gliding down until it was wrapped around her waist, his fingers just grazing the top of the ass.

His kiss and hold were relentless, forceful, but he simply couldn't let her go.

He didn't begin to relax until Erika's hands found their way to his shoulders, drifting higher as her fingers slipped through his hair, closing around it in tight fists. His scalp stung from her grip, but there was no way in hell he was going to complain.

Erika was kissing him back.

The passion between them ratcheted, soaring to levels he'd never reached. Kissing wasn't high on his foreplay list. There were too many other erogenous zones that brought him more pleasure, but goddamn if her kiss didn't leave his dick painfully hard, his balls tight.

Before he could think through his next move, he shifted them, the hand on her back sliding to her hip as he shoved one of his thighs between her legs. Erika pressed against him, dry humping his leg, the friction and heat from her pussy penetrating through her dress slacks and his lounge pants. Blake growled into her mouth, the hand on her hip aiding her motions, pushing and pulling her more firmly, helping to drive her arousal higher.

Fuck. Him.

She moaned into his mouth, the sexiest sound he'd ever heard. Blake deepened the kiss, determined to hear it again.

Erika didn't disappoint, giving him the same moan three more times. Her teeth found his lower lip, teasing it, biting it. She was playing with him, giving back as good as she got.

Blake released her nape, drawing his hand around to the front, lightly cupping her throat. He didn't apply pressure, just let her feel his touch, let the sheer possession of it sink into her psyche.

Erika wasn't a submissive. Not by a long shot. But he knew her well enough to read her responses. Her body's responses.

She liked it when he took charge, when he told her what to do. If he wasn't so worried she'd turn tail and run if he stopped kissing her, he'd slide his lips to her ears and give her some more of that dirty talk she was so fond of.

Blake lost sense of time, too wrapped up in the kiss, in the way Erika was riding his thigh, in *her*.

She was fucking everything.

Perfection.

And despite her assertions that they remain friends, he couldn't keep her in that box anymore. It was too small to contain what he wanted from her.

Which meant, he had to convince her to change her mind, to open her eyes and see what *he* saw.

That the two of them would be so fucking good together.

Hell, they'd be explosive.

Erika gasped in his mouth, her hips thrusting harder.

God, she was close to coming, just from dry humping his thigh.

Blake slid his hand to the opening of her slacks, intent on slipping his hand inside to find her clit. He knew without a doubt he could set her off like a bottle rocket within seconds.

His fingers brushed against her bare stomach, but damn if that touch wasn't the equivalent to someone dousing them in cold water.

Erika jerked back before he could read her intention. She almost stumbled in her attempt to escape him, so he reached out to grasp her arm, steadying her. That touch had her shrugging him off more firmly, retreating even farther away.

"Erik," he said softly, talking to her like she was a wild mare he was trying to tame.

"Blake." Her eyes were wide and wild, her cheeks red, her breathing stuttering.

He needed to do damage control, fast.

"Did you have enough time to think about Saturday night?" He was proud at how steady and strong his voice was.

She frowned. "What?"

"Sounded to me like you do your best thinking while kissing. Weren't you weighing over whether or not to invite Doug in while he was kissing you?"

She reached up, touching her kiss-swollen lips, which the alpha male inside took great pride in seeing. Erika was more than a little bit flustered, and he freaking liked that too. Liked keeping her on her toes. God knew that's where she'd had him the last few weeks.

"Tell you what, Erik. I'll make it easy on you. I'll pick you up at seven on Saturday."

Erika looked like she wanted to refuse, but when her shoulders slumped and she released a long breath, he knew he'd won.

She was too rattled to fight. He tucked that information away because that was something he could definitely use again.

"Okay," she said, slowly licking her lower lip, drawing his attention to it, making him want to resume the kissing right where they'd left off. His dick was rock-hard and hurting, and he suspected she was in a bit of pain herself. Stopping so close to coming couldn't have been easy for her.

"But it's not a date." She was trying to put parameters on this thing between them again.

Blake hated it, but because he didn't want to lose the ground he'd gained, didn't want to run the risk of pushing her too far, he merely said, "It is whatever we want it to be."

Two could play the vague game.

She looked like she wanted to belabor the point, to force him back into that "just friends" box. She was welcome to try, but he wasn't going back there without a fight. It was obvious she wasn't where he was, but Blake was nothing if not persuasive, and Erika had unwittingly given him way too much ammunition. There wasn't much about her he hadn't learned in the last three years, and he planned to put all that information to good use.

"You want Corky tonight?" he asked, even though it was technically his night to keep her.

Erika glanced around, spotting Corky lightly snoring in her dog bed in the living room. She shook her head. "No. She's comfy here."

Blake nodded once. "Okay."

Erika's gaze drifted lower, and Blake chuckled. There was no hiding the impact their kiss had on him. His erection was very obvious, thanks to his cotton lounge pants. He adjusted it as best he could while she watched.

When she realized he was looking at her, her gaze met his. He winked.

When she rolled her eyes good-naturedly, he decided he'd won that round. Erika was shaking her head as she turned and walked toward the door. The fact she wasn't stealing one last cuddle from Corky told him just how much he'd shaken her rafters.

Opening the door, she glanced over her shoulder. "Good night."

He managed to give her a carefree smile—though it took a bit of work. "Night, Erik."

Blake walked to his closed door, peering through the peephole to make sure she got back to her apartment okay. Twice, she paused, and he hoped like hell she would turn around.

If he'd known for sure she was coming back to expand on the kissing, he would throw the door open and take the decision away from her. Unfortunately, her halting steps could just as easily be her debating whether to come back and tell him she wasn't going to the party with him.

Rome wasn't built in a day, so Blake forced himself to remain where he was rather than take that risk.

Whatever internal debate she was waging ended when she unlocked the door to her apartment and went inside.

Knowing she was safe, Blake turned off the lights in the kitchen and living room, treading down the hallway to his bedroom, Corky hot on his heels. She leapt on the bed, assuming her usual spot, while he made his way to the bathroom. Staring in the mirror in front of the sink, he rested his palms on the counter, trying to take several deep breaths.

Then he reached inside his lounge pants and pulled out his cock, aware sleep wasn't happening until he took care of this.

Closing his eyes, he imagined a naked Erika bent over before him, her elbows resting on the sink.

She glanced over her shoulder at him. "Fuck me," she whispered.

Blake ran the head of his dick through her slit, her legs parted in invitation. Erika's pussy was hot and wet. "Hold on," he warned her. "I'm not going to take it easy on you."

She gave him a sexy smile. "Good," she taunted.

Blake grasped her hip with one hand, the other guiding him to her opening. He slammed inside with one fast, rough thrust that had him bottoming out. Her back arched as he white-knuckle gripped her hips, dragging her onto his cock before pushing her off again.

Erika's sexy sounds filled the bathroom as he fucked her harder than he'd ever fucked anyone before.

Reaching around her, he placed just three firm strokes on her clit before she came, her inner muscles clamping down so hard on his cock, he saw stars. Blake's climax erupted mere seconds after, and he filled her with his come.

Silently, he prayed for some strong swimmers, hoping tonight was the night he got his woman pregnant.

Blake gasped for breath, looking down at the mess he'd made, his come coating his fist and the basin of the sink.

Jesus.

What the fuck was *that*?

He'd never wanted to get a woman pregnant.

Hell, pregnancy was one of the reasons he'd never once had sex without a condom.

Now there was no denying just how different his feelings toward Erika were. She'd even twisted his jerk-off fantasies upside down and backward. Making him want so much more than sex for the first time in his life.

Blake stared at his reflection, feeling shell-shocked because he realized that with Erika…he wanted it all.

A best friend, a lover, a wife, a mother to his kids…

Forever.

He wanted forever with her.

Blake closed his eyes, debating whether it was better to let that word fade away or sink in deep.

Because Erika wasn't where he was, and there was a chance she never would be.

CHAPTER SIX

ERIKA PUT the wand back in the mascara and took one last look in the mirror.

She felt pretty.

And nervous.

Something she was becoming accustomed to when it came to Blake these days.

He'd been her best friend for so long that all shyness or discomfort or awkwardness between them faded ages ago. She should not be feeling nervous.

She considered wiping off her lipstick and going with a different shade. Then, she felt foolish for putting so much stock in her appearance when it was just *Blake*.

This wasn't even a date. She was doing him a favor because it sounded like he'd forgotten all about the charity event and couldn't find someone to go with him on such short notice. She figured she was his last-ditch effort, one that worked when he'd called in the IOU she'd offered after he'd picked her up from work.

She heard a single knock before her apartment door opened. The tap-tap-tap of doggie paws on her hardwood floor let her know exactly who'd arrived.

"Erik?" Blake yelled from the living room.

"Just a minute. I'm in the bathroom," she called out. "I'm almost ready."

Corky followed the sound of her voice, jumping against Erika, who quickly bent down to make sure the puppy's claws didn't snag her dress. "Hello, my sweetest," she said, picking up the wriggling dog but holding her at arm's length, twisting her face away. Puppy kisses and makeup didn't mix, so she put Corky down, the dog rushing back into her bedroom, no doubt in search of her favorite toy.

She'd delivered Corky to Blake this morning before she went to work, as he'd had a rare day off. He'd reminded her that he'd be here at seven, and a quick glance at her phone showed he was actually a few minutes early.

Fluffing her hair, she took a steadying breath and one last look in the mirror. She wasn't usually too fussed with her appearance. Not that she was a slob. It was just that she wasn't one of those women who primped in front of a mirror for hours on end. As far as Erika was concerned, a woman's worth had nothing to do with her looks and everything to do with her mind and her heart.

Until today anyway.

Today, she'd rushed home from the hospital, pissed about the fact she'd hit traffic. For the past two hours, she'd spent an ungodly amount of time stressing over her clothing, her hair, and her makeup.

Dammit.

Rolling her eyes at this ridiculous newfound vanity, she turned her back on her reflection and walked to her bedroom, grabbing the clutch she'd loaded with the essentials, transferred over from her larger daily purse. She'd only put her heels on a few minutes earlier, and her feet were already protesting. Doctors were experts when it came to practical, comfortable footwear, so while she owned lots of pretty heels, she didn't wear them very often.

Walking to the living room, she stopped short when she saw Blake leaning against the kitchen counter, looking at his phone. Both of their apartments had the same open floor plan. The kitchen, living room, and dining room all one huge room, sectioned off by an island counter. It was one of the things Erika had loved about the place. She didn't entertain often—most of her socializing was done at Blake's—but she liked how everyone was always sharing the same space, whether they were cooking, grabbing drinks from the fridge, or hanging out on the couch.

Blake looked like he'd stepped off the pages of *GQ*, giving his best James Bond impersonation, as his tuxedo fit him to perfection. The suit jacket showed off his broad, muscular shoulders, and he'd taken the time to tame his thick, shaggy, gorgeous black hair. He looked fucking hot. Which didn't help the butterflies that had taken residence in her stomach.

Blake glanced up when she entered, and that stupid vain woman practically swooned when his eyes widened in obvious appreciation. He gave her a wolf whistle as he tucked his phone into his jacket pocket and crossed the room to her.

"Holy shit, Erik."

She gave him a vogue pose, meant to make him laugh and hopefully break some of this tension she was feeling. Unfortunately, he didn't smile. Instead, he kept making his way toward her, reaching out to take one of her hands to spin her around.

"You're fucking gorgeous."

To hell with it. Tonight, she was going to embrace her inner narcissist, letting his compliments soak in.

"Thanks. You don't look so bad yourself." She reached out, fixing his tie, even though it was already perfect.

Blake was still looking at her, his eyes traveling from her hair, sliding along her curves—which she knew this dress accentuated just right—down to her heels and back again. "Suddenly regretting asking you to go with me tonight. Gonna have to beat my teammates off with a stick once they lay eyes on you in this dress."

She smiled. "Pretty sure that's not going to be a real concern."

"I'm pretty sure it is," he said, almost heatedly.

Erika didn't know if his compliments were just part of his charm or flirting schtick, but damn if they weren't working on her. She tried to dismiss what almost looked like jealousy flashing in his eyes as wishful thinking on her part, because why in the hell would Blake be jealous?

"A favor is a favor," she said, anxious to put them back on solid ground. "But I'm curious. Who were you going to take to this party if I was busy?"

He lifted one shoulder casually. "I would have gone stag. Partied with my teammates."

"Why didn't you do that anyway?"

"Because everything is more fun when you're there," he said, as if his words weren't the sweetest thing she'd ever heard.

"I have fun with you too." Her compliment felt lame on the heels of his, but he still lit up like a Christmas tree.

"I told Ashley that Corky will be here at your place. She has the spare key," Blake said. "I dropped it off this afternoon, but I'm starting to think it might be easier if we both just make her copies of her own."

"That's not a bad idea."

Ashley had proven herself to be as good a dog sitter as she was a babysitter. She'd been a godsend, taking care of Corky whenever they were both at work. Blake joked that their dog liked Ashley better than them.

"She's going to take her out in a couple hours for a walk, then she'll play with her for a little while, wear her out. Told her we should be back by midnight, and I'll take her out for her last walk then. Don't want Ash out with her too late," Blake finished.

"Sounds good."

Erika and Blake both gave Corky some goodbye snuggles, the two of them telling her to be a good girl, like there wasn't a thing weird about them talking to the dog like she could understand every word they said.

Blake helped her put on her coat, then offered his arm as they strolled to the elevators.

During the drive to the hotel, Erika's nerves settled. She'd obviously built tonight into something too big in her mind. Something that wouldn't have happened if Blake hadn't issued his invitation with that mind-blowing kiss of his.

She turned her face toward the passenger window, pretending to look at the stores they passed rather than let Blake see her flushed cheeks. Three days had passed, and she still couldn't think about that kiss without blushing like an innocent schoolgirl.

Of course, it had been a lot more than just a kiss. She still couldn't believe the way she'd reacted like a dog in heat, rubbing herself against his thick, powerful thigh. Erika had never responded to a kiss like that, never lost all sense of control. Not that Blake had helped. He'd been the one to shift her to that position, and his grip on her hips had certainly encouraged her to keep moving.

While she would never admit it aloud, she'd been damn close to coming. Just from dry humping his leg. She wouldn't have even thought that was a possibility until three nights ago.

Erika closed her eyes and shoved the memory of that night away. She had to, or else she wouldn't be able to face Blake.

This was three times now that the two of them had crossed into uncharted territory—at least for her. Between the masturbation lesson, the all-consuming kisses, and the leg humping, she was starting to have trouble recognizing herself in the mirror.

She'd never considered herself a particularly sexual woman. Her tastes in the bedroom always limited to the boring vanilla variety. Erika had never questioned if her disinterest in sex was because that was just the way she was wired. It's what she'd always assumed...but now she was wondering if the truth was, she'd never found a lover with enough skill to open her eyes to what she was missing.

Blake was definitely opening her eyes.

Of course he was.

Fate was having a good time with her these days.

After all, it had introduced her to Doug, a man whose interests, hopes, and dreams matched hers. Doug, like her, was looking for a long-term relationship with an eye toward marriage and kids. She should be turning cartwheels that she'd met him without having to keep slogging through online dating. The only problem she could find with Doug was that damn spark. It still hadn't flared, and the more time they spent together, the *less* physically attracted she became to him. She hadn't lied to Blake about letting that good-night kiss make the decision for her. It had been a perfectly nice—*ugh*—kiss, but in the end, it had left her cold rather than stirring her libido.

Fate had also flipped some switch in Blake that had him doing out-of-character things, with her following suit. Every time he was in the vicinity, so many damn sparks flickered and flared, she was shocked they hadn't burned down their building. She didn't even have to be with him. Just knowing he was across the hall turned her body into a sex compass, her tight nipples pointing toward her new north—Blake.

Being sexually attracted to her neighbor was becoming a big problem because, unlike Doug, Blake wasn't looking for anything more than a roll in the hay. Settling down in his mind seemed to be the equivalent to giving up, something Blake Wright never did.

She'd been right to insist that the two of them simply remain friends, and all the reasons she'd given him at the beginning were still there.

Sticking to her guns hadn't been an issue once in three years.

Not until now.

"You okay?" Blake reached across the console to touch her bouncing knee. "You're quiet."

She gave him what she hoped passed for an easy, breezy smile. "Just thinking about the next few weeks. I still have a lot of Christmas shopping to do." That wasn't a lie. The holidays were only a few weeks away, and Erika wasn't any better at buying presents than groceries, even though she had countless lists of who she was shopping for and gift ideas.

Blake nodded. "Tell you what. Why don't we check our schedules for next week and the two of us can dedicate one whole day to shopping and wrapping? Because I'm pretty behind as well."

She recalled they'd done the same thing last year, and it was the most prepared she had ever been for the holidays. "I'd like that."

He grinned. "Maybe we should make joint holiday shopping an annual event."

She nodded, aware that over the past few years, they'd established a lot of shared routines, including a spring-cleaning weekend shortly after the end of his season, where they tackled apartment projects together; double Thanksgivings that included lunch with her parents and dinner with his mom; and a trifecta Friendsgiving/Ugly Holiday Sweater/New Year's bash, always held on Christmas Eve due to the guys' hockey schedule.

"Here we are." Blake pulled up to the front of the hotel. "Wait there."

She remained where she was as Blake walked around the front of the car, handing the keys to the valet before opening the door for her. He helped her out, then tucked her hand in the crook of his arm again. It was a chilly night, as winter was starting to kick in, but it wasn't super cold. Regardless, she snuggled close enough that Blake must have thought she was seeking warmth because he dropped her hand and instead wrapped his arm around her shoulders, tugging her against his chest.

He was always warm, something she'd remarked on many times in the past. He claimed it was because his body was conditioned to the cold, which made sense, considering he spent so much of his time on ice.

"Blake," they heard someone call out as soon as they entered the ballroom. Glancing to the left, they spotted Tank and Preston standing next to one of the three bar setups.

Tank waved them over. "What's up, Doc? Didn't expect Blake to rope you into this dog and pony show. Thought he liked you."

She grinned. "Pulled the favor card."

Tank shook his head. "What a dick."

The two of them laughed.

"Only thing to do at crap like this," Tank added, "is get shit-faced."

He asked her what she wanted to drink, then ordered a red wine for her and beers for the guys. The four of them walked over to a table Blake's teammates had already claimed.

Glancing around, Erika instantly felt at ease, as she'd spent countless nights with all the guys at the table, and she was even familiar with one of the regular puck bunnies.

Coulton and Victor were sitting there, conversing quietly, as Preston reclaimed his seat, joining their discussion of—shocker—last night's game. It looked as if all three men had come stag. In fact, Tank appeared to be the only other guy who'd brought a date or, Jesus, *two* dates. Erika recognized one of the women, Lara, from celebrations at the pub and the hallway outside Blake's apartment following several victory sleepovers.

Tank introduced his other date, Emily, to Erika—joking that Preston had given him his plus one so he could bring "both his girls."

Erika noticed neither woman seemed bothered by his introduction, or unhappy that they were sharing the man.

Blake pulled out her chair, claiming the one next to her. Lara sat on his other side, giving Blake a sexy smile, despite the fact she was here with his best friend on the team. Tank and Blake exchanged pleasantries, clearly unbothered about the fact they were sitting between a woman they'd both taken to bed.

It didn't matter how many times she went out with Blake and his teammates; Erika would never get used to what she teasingly referred to as their Bedroom Roulette game.

Seeing the two women with Tank served as a good reminder to Erika why tonight wasn't a date, and why she and Blake were much better off as friends. She had too much pride to allow herself to become another notch on the sexy hockey star's bedpost.

"How long do we have to stay at this fucking fucked-up thing?" Victor grumbled. The defenseman's use of the F-word was so extreme and frequent, Erika couldn't recall ever hearing the man form a sentence that didn't use it at least once.

She bent her head, trying to hide her grin at his crankiness. She'd spent enough time around the grumpy man to know that Victor's bark was worse than his bite. His scowl was firmly in place tonight, letting everyone know he wasn't here out of the goodness of his heart, but due to his obligation to the team.

Tonight's charity, the Rays Foundation, provided money to foster children so that they could participate in school and community athletics. The foundation—sponsored by the Stingrays—paid for equipment, registration fees, and even provided transportation to practices and games, if necessary.

"It's for a good cause," Coulton reminded Victor. "So I don't mind too much. My Little Brother is one of the kids benefitting from the money raised tonight."

Coulton, the Rays' starting goalie, was physically huge, so when Erika first met him, she'd expected him to have a personality that matched. That didn't prove to be true at all, as Coulton was a soft-spoken, easygoing man who never seemed to get upset about anything. His nickname on the team was The Rock, as Coulton was their emotional rock, the one who always steadied the boat.

"I didn't know you had a brother," Lara remarked.

Tank shook his head as he wrapped his arm around his date's chair. "Coulton volunteers for Big Brothers Big Sisters. The Little

Brother thing is an honorary title. How long you been hanging with that kid now?"

Coulton smiled, clearly pleased by Tank's question. "Slade's been my Little Brother for about a year. Great kid. Lives with his aunt, but she's got five of her own, plus Slade's older sister, so he was getting lost in the crowd. His aunt enrolled him in the program when he started acting out at school, getting bad grades, shoplifting."

"How old is he?" Erika asked.

"Just turned eleven." Coulton beamed as he added, "Little punk actually made the honor roll this semester." If pride had a face, it would be Coulton's right now.

"You're changing that kid's life," Blake said, his words mirroring Erika's thoughts.

Coulton shrugged off the compliment, refusing to take any credit. "Kid is smart as shit. Just needed a little shove in the right direction. Talked to the director of the Rays Foundation about him. Slade wants to try out for little league baseball in the spring."

"Fucking baseball," Victor scoffed. "Why aren't you getting the kid into hockey?"

Coulton snorted. "I've tried but he's ornery as shit. Determined to be a major league baseball pitcher."

"You're gonna be fucked if you have to sit through endless innings of the most boring fucking game in the history of fucking sports," Victor persisted.

"Hockey's not for everyone, Vic," Preston chimed in diplomatically…and without cursing.

Victor grumbled under his breath while the rest of them laughed, accustomed to and amused by his disdain for basically everything.

They all quieted down as the director of the Rays Foundation approached the podium, thanking them for their attendance while directing their attention to one side of the room, where countless silent auction items were being displayed. Once the director finished her spiel, she nodded at the kitchen door, apparently the signal for dinner to be served.

Conversation at the table flowed as they worked their way through the salad, dinner, and dessert courses.

Victor's patience for the event ran out before dessert, so he slipped out, claiming he had an early morning breakfast date with his niece, Phillipa. Erika had met Victor's young niece—Pip, as he called her—a couple of times at team picnics, and it was obvious Victor doted on the four-year-old, who had her gruff uncle wrapped around her little finger.

After the meal, she and Blake wandered along the tables with the silent auction items, placing bids more in an attempt to increase the donations than because they actually wanted to win. Once the dishes were cleared, a popular local band began playing, and Erika found herself swept out onto the floor, dancing in a wide circle of Stingrays players and their dates, laughing as Blake spun her around to several fast-paced covers.

They returned to the table, in need of a break and water, followed by Tank, Lara, and Emily. Preston and Coulton were still sitting there, nursing their beers, neither man interested in dancing.

"Hey, guys," a female voice said.

"What's up, Mouse?" Tank asked as Erika turned around, looking for the speaker. Apparently, Tank's standard greeting for Erika was his standard for everyone. All he did was switch the nicknames.

The woman approached their table, shooting Tank a somewhat surprised look.

"You know McKenna?" Blake asked Tank, inviting the petite brunette to join them. "Thought you avoided the administrative offices like the plague."

Tank, who did seem to spend a fair amount of time in trouble for his flamboyant behavior off the rink and due to inappropriate comments made during interviews, flipped Blake the bird, ignored the question, then started kissing Lara.

McKenna winced at Tank's rude gesture.

"Erik, this is McKenna Bailey. She just started working for the Rays as our social media manager a few months ago. McKenna, this is my neighbor, Dr. Erika Nelson."

McKenna pushed up her thick-rimmed glasses as she reached out to shake Erika's hand. "Nice to meet you. I thought you were a guy when Blake told me he'd adopted a puppy with his neighbor, Erik. To be honest, when you said that, I kind of thought you were gay," she said, glancing at Blake.

The table erupted in laughter, everyone cracking up over McKenna's comment.

"Oh my God. Blake…gay!" Erika laughed so hard, tears streamed from her eyes. "That's hilarious."

Blake must have felt the need to flex his heterosexual muscles because he wrapped his arm around Erika's waist, pulling her tightly against him before dropping a kiss on the side of her head. "It's not *that* damn funny." Turning back to McKenna, he said, "Erik is my nickname for her."

"Sorry. It's just…" McKenna flushed bright red, clearly embarrassed either by her mistaken impression or the fact she'd blurted it out. "Blake's shown me a lot of pictures of Corky. She's so adorable," McKenna gushed to Erika.

Erika was amused to hear Blake was showing off their puppy at work. Not that it surprised her. She'd watched him whip out his phone at the grocery store to show complete strangers pictures of Corky.

Tank seemed less amused. "He's got a million pictures of that dog on his phone. I swear to God, I've seen fewer photos of Elio Moretti's newborn daughter than that damn dog. And Elio's lost his mind over that baby."

Elio, a former teammate, had retired from hockey at the end of the previous season, shocking everyone with a quick wedding to a woman no one even knew he'd been dating. A few months after the wedding, the baby was born.

Blake rolled his eyes, scowling at Tank. "Who hurt you, man?" he joked, referring to Tank's apparent lack of a soul. Erika had always considered Blake to be a playboy—until she'd met Tank. At which point she realized she needed a sliding scale in terms of bad boy levels.

Blake was on the scale, but only at level one. Meanwhile, Tank was on the top tier, completely on his own, as he kept redefining the word playboy for Erika with his actions. The fact the man had unapologetically brought two dates to the same function had her rethinking the definition yet again. Erika couldn't help but be curious if Tank was also planning to sleep with both women tonight.

McKenna flashed Tank a confused look, taking in the fact he had his arms wrapped both around Lara's and Emily's shoulders. She seemed to be trying to figure out which woman was his date. Like most normal women, it didn't seem to occur to McKenna he was there with both.

"Do you guys mind if I snap a picture of you for the socials?" McKenna asked, redirecting her attention to the rest of the table.

"Sure," Coulton said good-naturedly. "How do you want us?"

McKenna moved them all to one side of the table, Preston, Coulton, Blake, and Erika sitting together, as Tank and his two dates stood behind them, the women hanging on Tank, who was grinning from ear to ear.

God only knew how McKenna was going to caption that photo. She thanked them all after snapping a few pics, shooting sideways glances at Tank, who was kissing Lara as Emily playfully toyed with his bowtie, apparently waiting for her turn for some hardcore PDA.

"Um...okay, then," McKenna said, adjusting her glasses again. "I need to keep working the room."

She walked away, casting a couple of looks over her shoulder.

"She seems like a nice girl," Erika said.

Blake nodded. "She is." Turning his attention to Coulton and Preston, he added, "One of you should ask her out."

Coulton shook his head. "Not my type."

Erika waited for him to expound on that, but he didn't. When Blake didn't press, it was obvious he agreed, leaving her to wonder what kind of woman would catch Coulton's eye. Given his gentle disposition, she definitely thought McKenna, who seemed very sweet, if just a tiny bit awkward, might be perfect for him.

Preston also rejected the idea. "I've already met my perfect woman."

Blake rolled his eyes. "Jesus, man. Seriously?"

Erika frowned. "Did I miss something?"

Preston sighed. "I went to a holiday kickoff party in Philly a couple weekends ago with Elio. Met this woman, Chelsea." Preston smiled as he said her name, like it was the greatest word ever spoken. "We really connected. Spent the whole night talking and dancing and…"

He tried to let his silence fill in the blanks, but Tank couldn't resist joining the conversation. "And fucking."

Preston scowled. "Fucking isn't the word I'd use."

"Aw, jeez, Romeo," Coulton mumbled.

Erika giggled. Preston was the team romantic, the guy seriously in love with the concept of love. Obviously, he took exception to Tank's description because if Preston was as enamored of the woman as he appeared, he would never use such a coarse word.

"So you and Chelsea are dating? Going to do a long-distance relationship between Philadelphia and Baltimore?" Erika asked, wondering why the woman wasn't here, if that was the case.

Preston shook his head. "No. She left."

"Left?"

"The country. She flew to Paris to work in a famous design house. She's in fashion," Preston added.

"Wow. Cool job," Erika murmured.

"Basically," Tank said, placing his hand on Preston's shoulder and giving it a squeeze, "our Romeo here is brokenhearted because his dream woman moved halfway across the world right after their one-night stand."

"Oh no. I'm sorry, Preston."

Preston took a swig of his beer, staring at the nearly empty bottle a second before tipping it back and draining it. "If it's meant to be, it'll be."

"Not trying long-distance like Erika suggested?" Blake asked.

"No. Not at all. It's just...she's my soul mate. I know it. So I have to have faith that fate will bring her back to me."

"Like a serendipity thing?" Erika asked.

Preston shrugged. "I know it sounds crazy. It's just...Chelsea was..."

"I think it sounds wonderful," she reassured him, even though she feared Preston might be facing heartbreak somewhere down the line.

The band started playing a slow song, and she found herself being pulled out of her chair by Blake. She followed him to the floor, trying to ignore how good it felt to be wrapped in his strong arms.

"Tired of sharing you with my teammates," he grumbled.

She gave him a breathy laugh. "We were just talking."

"They're monopolizing you."

She pulled away at his grumpy tone, about to tease him and tell him he sounded like Victor, but when she saw his frown, she realized he was being sincere.

Erika decided her best response was to change the subject. "Thank you for inviting me tonight. It's been a lot of fun."

His frown lines faded, replaced with a smile. "Thank you for coming. I know it was last-minute."

Blake's hand stroked up and down her back a few times

before stopping at the nape of her neck, his large hand lightly gripping her there. He'd held her that way a few times now, and every single time, her body responded to it the same way. Her nipples budding, her pussy clenching, her stomach fluttering.

She wrapped her arms around his waist more tightly, resting the side of her head on his chest, slowly swaying to the band's cover of Justin Bieber's "Anyone." While Erika had never succumbed to Bieber fever, she really did like this song.

Blake placed a kiss on the side of her head. In her mind, she kept trying to tell herself it was a perfectly friendly, platonic kiss, but her body was interpreting it in a much different way.

Erika smiled when he started humming along to the song. He tried to sing a bit of the chorus but messed up the words. She tilted her head back to look at him. "You realize the words aren't that complicated."

Blake chuckled. "Maybe not, but it's not 'Enter Sandman' either. I can scream-sing every word of that song."

She rolled her eyes. "I've seen that performance before. Not interested in an encore." One night after pizza, the guys started scrolling through Tank's workout playlist while playing a drinking game. As if they'd planned it, the second that song came on, every Rays player broke out singing, playing air electric guitars and drums and swinging their heads around like lunatics. It was hilarious, but it sure as shit didn't make Erika like the song any better.

They continued swaying to the slow song, Blake's hands exploring with reckless abandon, caressing her back, gripping her waist, stroking her hair. It was the most tactile dance of her life, and it was wreaking havoc on her willpower...and her libido.

When the song ended, she wasn't sure whether to be relieved or depressed because Blake released her, clasping hands with her to lead her back to the table. They hung out for a little while longer, chatting with Preston and Coulton, as Tank and his dates did a sexy three-way bump and grind on the dance floor.

"Had enough?" Blake asked, leaning close.

She nodded.

The two of them said their goodbyes, and he wrapped his arm around her shoulders as they waited for the valet to bring the car.

Once they were tucked into his Audi, the heater blasting warm air on high, Erika twisted to look at Blake. "Is Tank planning on sleeping with both those women tonight?"

Blake glanced her direction, grinning. "Yes."

The answer was too simple, and Blake knew it. Just like she knew he was trying to get a rise out of her.

"Fine," she finally snapped. "I'll bite. How exactly does that work?"

Blake chuckled. "The usual way, but with three bodies in the bed. You have to understand that Lara and Emily are into each other as well. So while Tank will definitely fuck both of them, the women will be enjoying each other at the same time."

Erika frowned. "Have you…ever…"

Blake didn't bother to hold back his loud laughter. "Good God, no. But I like that you think I'm a big enough stud to pull it off."

She snorted.

"I don't share, Erik. When I'm with a woman, I want all her focus on me because she can be damn sure all my focus will be on her."

Erika recalled the night of his "lesson." None of her past boyfriends had ever been so in tune with her body, her needs, her desires. Blake had proven himself to be a master when it came to the female body, but more than that, he'd been an expert on *hers*, specifically.

"So are you going to keep seeing Doug?" Blake asked.

He had a way of saying Doug's name, drawing it out, that made it sound like the name itself was the most ridiculous one he'd ever heard.

Erika nodded. "Yeah. We have a good time and…" She

paused, refusing to say Doug was a nice guy again, even though he was. She should put some effort into thinking of better descriptors, but unfortunately, every time she pictured Doug in her mind, the only word that came to her was *nice*.

"Still no sex yet?"

He knew the answer to that question. After all, he'd stopped her before she could invite Doug in the other night, and she hadn't seen him since.

She should tell him to mind his own damn business, but given the conversations they'd had over the past month or so, it seemed that the last barrier to full disclosure in their friendship had fallen.

"Nope. Not yet," she replied.

Blake looked pensive when he glanced her way again. "Why not?"

"Because, unlike you, I don't fuck on the first date."

He smirked. "Maybe not, but you and Doug," he drawled out the damn name again, "have been on a lot of dates."

"Six dates is not a lot of dates," she pointed out.

"It's a record for you."

She sighed, realizing how sad that truth was. "I'm just taking things slow."

Erika expected Blake to make some joke about her going overboard on the slow thing, but instead, she got the sense he approved.

Parking near their building, Blake opened her door for her, the two of them walking inside arm in arm. "I'll grab Corky and take her out before bed," Blake offered, following her into her apartment.

Corky, as always, was waiting for them, her tail wagging a million miles an hour as she yapped happily. Erika kicked off her shoes by the door, a bad habit she'd accepted long ago that she would never break. One of these days she was going to invest in a shoe caddy to keep by the front door. Her heels were added to the current pile of shoes residing there, which included her running shoes and the flats she'd worn to work today. She was sort of surprised Corky hadn't used any of them as chew toys.

Blake trailed behind her as she walked to the kitchen.

"Want some coffee?" she offered. "I think I have some decaf pods."

He nodded. "Sounds good. While you make it, I'll walk Cork." Blake grabbed Corky's leash from the hook she'd hung by the door, while Erika put a pod in the machine and pressed the button to brew the first cup. Then she headed to her bedroom, quickly stripping off her dress and putting on her comfies. She tugged on a soft cotton long-sleeve tee and pajama bottoms, adding fuzzy socks to keep her feet warm.

She'd just finished adding the creamer to their coffees when Blake returned.

"You changed," he said.

Erika handed him the cup of coffee. "Getting dressed up is fun...for a little while. These pajamas are a hell of a lot more comfortable."

Blake set his cup on the counter without taking a sip. Instead, he reached out, grasping her waist and pulling her close to him. "I was hoping to strip you out of your dress."

She blinked a couple of times, trying to figure out if she'd heard him right. Before she could question him, he pressed his lips against hers in a kiss that was as hot and hungry as the one he'd given her a few days earlier.

This time, Erika was better prepared. Placing her hands against his chest, she pushed until he broke the kiss.

"Erik," he murmured, clearly unhappy about stopping.

"You can't keep kissing me," she said, wishing her voice sounded less breathy.

He narrowed his eyes. "Our kisses haven't been one-sided, you know. You've been kissing me back."

"I know," she conceded. "But I shouldn't have. Blake, all the reasons we had for not going out three years ago are still there. God," she said, running her fingers through her hair. "If anything, there are even more reasons. We've become friends, best friends, and we have Corky. I'm not going to deny I'm attracted to you, but…" She could see Blake composing a whole list of arguments, ready to fight her. She couldn't let him. "But I'm dating Doug now. He's perfect for me, and I really want to give our relationship a chance."

The desire she'd seen in Blake's eyes faded. It appeared she'd offered the one argument he couldn't refute.

It was a shame it was a lie.

The more time she spent with Doug—and Blake—the more she could see Doug wasn't the one. While she hated that she was putting so much stock in sparks, she couldn't help wanting a man who offered the best of both worlds, someone who wanted a long-term committed relationship, who also knocked her socks off in bed.

"Why don't you keep Corky at your place tonight," she added, desperate to bring this night to a close. "You're headed out on the road for a couple of days and you won't get to see her."

Blake hesitated, and Erika held her breath, praying he would let this conversation end here.

She needed some distance from him to…

Well, to think.

Erika wasn't an impulsive person, so she really needed time to make sense of everything that had happened between her and Blake, to determine how she could avert any more mishaps. And so she could analyze all the dates and conversations and make rational, smart decisions about Doug.

Mercifully, Blake pushed away from the counter, bending down to scoop up Corky, who'd been prancing around their ankles.

"Night, Erik."

His tone was gruff and…God…a bit angry. She chose to pretend she couldn't hear it.

"Good night," she said with a lightness she didn't feel. "Thanks again."

When the door closed behind him, she deflated, all the air seeping out of her body as her foolish head and stupid heart started playing out a different ending to the night.

One where Blake really did strip her out of her dress, lead her to the bedroom, and give her more of those amazing orgasms.

To quote Victor…she was fucking fucked.

CHAPTER SEVEN

BLAKE LEANED back in his chair, taking a sip of his beer, letting his teammates and friends party around him. He should have skipped the damn celebration because he was a buzzkill.

While the Rays won tonight, it hadn't been because of anything *he'd* done. Hell, if anything, they'd won despite him. His head hadn't been in the game because all he could think about was Erika—who was out with Doug again.

Nearly a week had passed since he'd tried to kiss her good night after the charity event. Truth was, he'd been hoping to do a shit-ton more than just kiss her. He'd planned to do exactly what he'd said. Strip her out of that sexy dress of hers, kiss her senseless, then drag her back to her bedroom to—

"What the hell is wrong with you tonight?" Tank claimed the seat next to him. "You've been in a foul mood since walking into the arena. We won the game, dude. It's time to eat, drink, and fuck."

Blake shook his head. "We won by the skin of our teeth, and it's not like I have anything to celebrate. I stunk it up big-time."

"So you couldn't find the back of the net. Happens to all of us," Tank reassured him.

Blake lifted one shoulder, not really interested in rehashing the game. The only reason they hadn't had their asses handed to them was because Coulton was on fucking fire. Boston had twice the shots on goal they'd had, and Coulton had stopped every freaking one. Their goalie was catching pucks in midair like they were punches someone was swinging at his mother. Nothing got by him. Not a single goddamn thing.

The crazy thing was, Blake had gotten the impression Coulton had arrived for the game every bit as pissed off as he was. However, while Blake had served up a fucking pizza in the middle of the third that gave Boston a serious chance to score, Coulton had been their MVP, shutting them down hard at every turn.

Blake glanced around Pat's Pub. "Where's Coulton?"

"Said he had something to take care of," Tank said. "I told him after the way he played tonight, Padraig would probably give him every round for free, but the dude was in as much of a mood as you are. What happened? Did your menstrual cycles sync up?"

Blake smirked. "You're a dick."

"And you're killing my buzz. What's wrong?" Tank asked again.

"Erika is out on a date."

Tank frowned, confused by his response. "So?"

"So, I think she's really into this guy. Doug," he added, the man's name tasting like manure anytime he was forced to say it.

Tank studied his face for a few seconds, then slapped him on the back. "It's about damn time. Hey, Preston, Victor. Come here," Tank called out, waving their teammates and buddies over.

"What's going on?" Preston asked.

Tank tilted his head in Blake's direction. "Einstein here finally figured it out."

Victor's and Preston's expressions were blank until Tank added, "Erika."

Preston smiled widely. "It's about damn time," he said, echoing Tank's exact words.

"What's that supposed to mean?" Blake asked.

"It means you've had the hots for her since about five minutes after she moved in," Preston pointed out.

Blake hadn't exactly hidden his interest in Erika when they'd first met, so it wasn't like that was news. "I know. And she shot me down because she's always been looking for a relationship, and I'm not."

"Jesus," Tank muttered, shaking his head.

Blake's temper had been skating just under the surface all night, so the fact they were saying a bunch of shit that didn't make sense wasn't helping. "If you have something to say, just say it!"

Victor gave him a look. "That woman has been your fucking girlfriend for three years. You've just been too fucking stupid to see it."

Blake scowled. "No, she hasn't."

Tank rolled his eyes. "Man, I love you like a brother, but you can be blind sometimes. You and Erika eat dinner together at least three times a week. You keep food in each other's refrigerators. You bring her to every single party, every pizza and game night, and even last week's fundraiser."

"You go to the grocery store together, spend holidays together," Preston chimed in. "You have coffee with her almost every morning, go running with her in the off-season."

Tank swiped at his phone screen, pointing to a picture of Corky. "You adopted a fucking *dog* together, for God's sake."

"She's your fucking *girlfriend*," Victor growled, repeating himself. "A girlfriend without benefits, which is totally fucked up."

"We *all* agree that's pretty fucked," Tank added.

Blake listened as they rattled off their lists, dumbfounded by how right they were. He leaned forward, resting his forehead in his hand. "She's my girlfriend," he muttered.

Tank slapped him on the shoulder again, like he was congratulating him for doing something great, rather than finally opening his eyes to something that should have been obvious. "She's a great girl. We all love her, and she's perfect for you, man."

Preston nodded. "The two of you are good for each other."

"She's a hell of a lot better than Mindy," Victor added. "I don't know how the fuck you can stand that woman's fucking grating voice and laugh." While Blake, Tank, and Preston—pre-Chelsea—had always enjoyed the company of puck bunnies, Victor had never invited a single Rays groupie home with him.

"Erika is great," Blake said miserably.

"What's wrong?" Preston said.

"She's out with another man. *Doug*," Blake spat out. "I think it might be getting serious."

"So fucking make it unserious," Victor proposed, as if that was a simple solution. "She's *your* fucking girlfriend. You gonna let some douchebag take her out?"

Tank gestured toward Victor like every word he'd said was pure genius. Not that Blake was surprised. Victor and Tank were bulldozers, neither man shy when it came to getting what they wanted.

Blake glanced over at Preston, expecting him to be the voice of reason, but he was nodding as well.

"She's your soul mate," Preston said. "I could see that right from the beginning."

Victor rolled his eyes, just like he always did when Preston started talking about true love and soul mates. "I need another fucking beer before Romeo here starts reciting poetry." He stood, looking around the table. "Who else?"

Tank stood as well. "Let's get another round for the table. We need to come up with a plan of attack for our guy here."

Blake appreciated his friends' support, and if Erika was sitting at home right now with Corky, he would have already blown out of this place, driving straight home to clue her in on the girlfriend thing.

Another teammate called out Preston's name, calling him over to ask him to repeat some funny story.

Preston gave him a questioning look.

"Go ahead," Blake said. "I'm fine."

Preston rose, grabbing his beer to join the other conversation.

Blake took another swig of beer then winced. He'd been sitting here with his head up his ass for so long that the beer had gone warm. Putting it back down on the table, he tried to figure out when things had changed between him and Erika. Because, despite his teammates' assertions, she hadn't *always* been his girlfriend.

Sifting through the past three years, he had to admit that once she'd shot his flirting down, insisting they weren't going to be anything more than friends, the friendship blossomed fast. While he would concede to the idea that she was his girlfriend now in almost every way, Blake didn't think that was true the first year they'd been neighbors.

Nope, the tide had turned somewhere in these past couple of years, as they'd grown closer. He couldn't put his finger on exactly when. Maybe there wasn't an exact day and time, but his friends were right. He'd unwittingly put her in the role of his girlfriend, leaning on her when he needed bolstering, seeking her out when he needed advice or an opinion, taking care of her when she forgot to feed herself.

He grinned slightly when he realized Victor calling Erika his girlfriend hadn't bugged him at all. He'd always proclaimed loudly—and to anyone who would listen—that he was happy with his footloose and fancy-free lifestyle. Now, he could see his happiness wasn't driven by the fact he was single.

Nope.

He was happy because he already had Erika in his life. She was the first person he thought of when he opened his eyes and the last one he thought of before falling asleep. And he was ashamed to admit that was true even on nights when he wasn't alone...because somewhere along the line, he'd started comparing the women he slept with to his neighbor as well. He was certain that was why his attraction to Mindy had waned. She simply couldn't hold a candle to Erika.

"Fuck," he muttered, throwing his head back. None of these revelations were helping improve his mood. If anything, he was in worse shape now than when he'd walked into Pat's Pub. Because admitting his feelings to himself—even though it had taken him too damn long—was the easy part.

Erika was going to be much harder to convince. For that laundry list of reasons she constantly threw out at him. She wasn't willing to risk their friendship on what she assumed would be a roll in the hay. And why *wouldn't* she assume that was all it would be? His track record had been on display for three full years, proving that when it came to serious relationships, he meant what he said about being disinterested.

How could he convince her that she was the exception?

And even if he did, had he waited too long? She was on date number seven with Doug, and after the way she so easily pushed Blake away after the fundraiser, he feared that meant she really *was* serious about the other man, ready to take the next step in their relationship.

He looked at the clock on his phone. It was close to midnight. Which meant, chances were good her date was over.

Or...it had gone into overtime.

In her bedroom.

The thought of Doug touching and kissing his girl had Blake seeing red, irritating him enough that he considered driving home and banging on her door to interrupt anything that might be happening.

Yeah. That would go over like a lead balloon.

Regardless, he rose, struggling to hold back his inner caveman. The one beating his chest and itching for a fight.

Before he could act on that thought, two things happened

simultaneously. His phone rang, and Mindy spotted him, aware he was about to make his escape.

Blake answered the phone the second he saw Erika's name on the screen.

"Erik," he said.

Unfortunately, at the same time, Mindy rushed over. "Blake!" she squealed. "It's time to celebrate!"

"Blake," Erika said.

He knew in an instant something was wrong.

* * *

Erika stood by a tree, desperately fighting back tears as she watched Corky do her business. Tonight had been a clusterfuck from the word go, and now things had gone from bad to worse.

Her date with Doug had been fine—another word as boring as *nice*—and for a little while, she'd debated if she was being unfair, assuming sex with Doug would be uneventful without giving him a chance to prove her wrong. Maybe the sparks that weren't coming with his kisses would appear in the bedroom.

Sure, Blake practically set her hair on fire with just a touch, but was it fair to compare Blake—a freaking sex god—to a mere mortal?

And while she hadn't had actual sex with Blake, he'd already proven himself to be the best she'd ever had.

How sad was that statement about her sex life? That Blake had rocked her world harder with a dildo and a dry hump than the men she'd gone all the way with.

She closed her eyes, warding off unwanted thoughts and feelings.

So *what* if Blake was great in the bedroom? She needed more than that.

She and Doug were compatible, like-minded, and they had a good time. Or a good enough time. It wasn't like it was a lot of over-the-top laughter and fun, like she shared with Blake, but their dates had been pleasant.

She mentally added *pleasant* to her list of shitty descriptors.

By the time she and Doug had left the movie theater tonight, Erika had made up her mind to invite him in.

However, when he parked the car by the curb outside her building, her words evaporated. Doug gave her a long, slow kiss, and as always, Erika's thoughts wandered back to Blake. To the passion, the hunger, the sheer need behind his kisses.

Doug kissed her like he was trying to win points by impressing her with his technique, all suave finesse and a gentleness that almost put her to sleep.

Blake kissed her like she fucking mattered, like she was the air, the water, the food he needed to survive, and without her lips, he'd die.

By the time their kiss ended, she'd changed her mind about sleeping with Doug—he'd given her too much time to think during the boring buss—and she had repeated the same words she'd used at the end of every single one of their dates. She'd thanked him for a lovely evening, then lied about having an early morning.

At the beginning, Doug had taken her dismissals with good grace, but that polish had become a little more tarnished every time she'd sent him away with nothing more than a few kisses. She hadn't even let him get to second base and cop a feel.

Tonight, he hadn't smiled and said good night. He'd scowled, point-blank asking her if the two of them were "ever going to fuck."

His words had pissed her off. When she told him she wasn't going to be pressured into something she wasn't ready for, he'd called her a prude and told her to get out of his car, skidding his tires in his haste to get away from her.

She tried to convince herself she'd made a lucky break, that Doug obviously wasn't the man she'd thought he was, but her guilty conscience kept rearing its head, suggesting that, number one, she hadn't really given Doug a fair shot, and number two, she probably shouldn't have kept going on dates with him if she wasn't truly interested.

The thing was, she *thought* she should be interested because of all those stupid "we're well-suited" reasons that had seemed so fucking important at the beginning. Now, she was starting to wonder if she'd been using Doug as a buffer, as a way to keep Blake at arm's length.

Because she was in serious danger of giving in to her best friend's desire to take her to bed, even though she knew doing so would be the biggest mistake of her life.

Blake didn't do commitment, didn't do girlfriends, didn't want marriage for at least twenty more years. She didn't even know if he wanted kids. Worse than that, he lived across the hall.

She knew exactly how the whole thing would play out. She'd succumb to his charms, they'd have amazing sex for one, two, maybe even a few nights. And then, when he was done, Mr. Casual would expect things to return to normal, which meant, she'd be forced to pretend he hadn't broken her heart while watching puck bunny after puck bunny leave his apartment every morning.

Erika would probably try to maintain the friendship—for Corky's sake—but in the end, she'd lose the battle, they'd have some huge blowout fight, and eventually the strain would get so bad that she'd have to move out of the apartment she loved.

And even knowing all of that wasn't helping her resist him. Because his kisses, his charming smiles, and his wicked, teasing touches, combined with the way he genuinely cared about her, was all too much.

Her emotional breakdown was interrupted when a flash of lightning split the sky, followed by a huge crack of thunder.

"Shit!" Erika jumped, raising her hands to cover her ears at the same time, Corky jolted.

Erika heard a snap and felt the leash go slack—then Corky sprinted across the grassy park area behind their building.

The grassy, *unfenced* area.

"Corky!" she screamed, taking off after the dog as the skies opened, a heavy downpour soaking her to the skin in less than a minute.

Another flash of lightning struck, and she stumbled when a loud rumble of thunder boomed overhead. Her heart was racing, more from fear than exertion, and she panicked when Corky disappeared through a small grove of trees. Her apartment complex maintained the commons for residents, and while there had been some talk of adding a fenced-off dog park area, that hadn't happened yet.

"Corky," she yelled again, tears mixing with the rain streaming down her cheeks. She couldn't see the dog at all anymore, the night and the heavy rain limiting her view.

"Please," she cried. "Oh God, please, Corky. Come back!" True terror took hold when another loud roar of thunder cut through the night, and Corky was nowhere in sight.

She continued running, yelling the dog's name, but every time another flash of lightning struck or thunder boomed, her fear continued to grow until it was nearly paralyzing.

A sob fell from her throat, opening the floodgates as she raced around, desperately searching for Corky.

Blake.

She needed Blake.

Erika pulled out her phone. He hadn't been home when she returned for her date, which meant, he'd probably gone out with the team following tonight's game. Either to celebrate or drown his sorrows. Once again, she'd missed the game. She had no idea if they'd won or lost.

Fumbling with her cell, she opened her contacts and hit his number. Mercifully he answered after just two rings.

"Erik," she heard him say, the noise in the background proving her guess about him going out with his friends.

"Blake! It's time to celebrate!"

Erika would recognize Mindy's voice anywhere. The idea that he was out with the other woman only added to her pain.

"Blake," she said, her voice hoarse. She swallowed heavily. "Please." The second she said the word, she started crying again.

"What's wrong, Erik? Where are you?"

"Park…behind…the building." Every word she spoke was broken by a loud gasp for breath. "Corky," she said, her voice breaking.

The noise behind Blake faded, and she thought she heard a horn honk. He must have left the bar. "What happened?"

She was grateful for the strength in his voice, the steadiness of his tone. Considering she was completely falling apart, it was good *one* of them was able to function.

"She broke free from the leash. The thunder scared her. I can't find her. I can't find her!" she repeated, still tromping around the area, zigzagging from one end of the park to the next, perfectly aware the dog had kept running. She could be down any of the dark streets surrounding them.

Why hadn't they gotten her chipped at the vet?

"I'm on my way now." She heard his car start, and she prayed he'd been at Pat's Pub because it was the closest bar to their building.

Another flash of lightning lit the sky, and she screamed.

"Jesus, Erik…calm down, baby. I'll be there as quick as I can. It's going to be okay. We'll find her."

She'd never told Blake about her fear of storms because the catalyst for that phobia was a story she wasn't proud of. Blake only knew the super-straight, rule-follower Erika, and she'd never filled him in on her early wild-child reputation, ashamed of who she used to be.

"I was trying to take her out before the storm started," she said. "But I got distracted." By thoughts of him and Doug and how she was screwing up her life.

Blake stayed on the line with her while he drove home, his calm voice soothing her enough that she was able to stop crying.

They hung up when, ten minutes later, she saw him sprinting across the grassy field toward her. Erika ran to him, meeting him halfway, so grateful when he wrapped his arms around her, comforting her.

"It's okay, Erik. It's okay," he soothed, even as he surveyed the area in search of Corky. "Which direction did she go?"

Erika pointed, and he grasped her hand, the two of them moving rapidly in that direction.

"There aren't many places for her to hide in the park," he pointed out, something Erika might have realized if she hadn't let her terror take over.

They crossed the street, walking toward the row houses there. Most had shrubs adorning their front stoops.

Blake stopped when they reached the middle, glancing around them. Then he put two fingers in his mouth and blew, his whistle loud.

Corky was trained to respond to it, always racing to him. Erika had been impressed by the trick, even though it wasn't one she could mimic. She couldn't whistle to save her soul.

When Corky didn't appear, Blake did it again as they both looked down the street.

Erika squinted, pointed to a large bush three houses away. "I think I see a flash of white!"

She and Blake rushed over to the bush, Blake reaching into his coat pocket to pull out a plastic container of Corky's favorite treats. "Stopped for dog food and treats this afternoon on the way to the game. It was still in my car."

He shook the jug, Corky's favorite sound, and Erika heard it. A whimper.

They squatted down, Blake pushing some of the limbs aside, allowing them to see Corky cowering behind the bush.

"There you are, pretty girl." Blake opened the jug and shook several of the bite-sized treats into his large palm. "You don't like the rain any more than your mommy, do you?"

Whatever fear Corky might have been experiencing, it

vanished when presented with a handful of treats. She crawled out from her hiding spot, happily jumping up, her paws leaving muddy prints on Blake's jacket.

He scooped the puppy into his arms, tucking her securely under his coat, then wrapped his arm around Erika's shoulders.

"Jesus, Erik, you're drenched and shivering. Let's get you inside where it's warm."

She hadn't noticed how badly she was shaking, and while she was chilly, it was fear causing her to tremble so violently, not the cold.

They quickly made their way back to the building, taking the elevator to their floor. Even though she was out of the rain, Erika's shaking worsened and her teeth started chattering.

Blake watched her, concern in his eyes.

Grabbing her hand, he tugged her toward his apartment, the three of them leaving puddles as they walked straight through the living room and down the hall to Blake's bedroom. She paused in the doorway, but he propelled her forward with a firm hand on her lower back. "Bathroom."

She was too numb and tired to resist when he guided her into his en suite. He grabbed a large, fluffy bath towel and handed it to her before placing Corky on the sink counter.

"Dry her off," Blake directed. She wasn't sure why *he* wasn't drying the dog, considering his hands were much steadier.

Regardless, she did as he asked, the action soothing some of her rougher edges. Corky was here, safe and sound. The puppy's tail wagged, and she kept trying to lick the raindrops sliding down Erika's hands. Despite being inside, her clothing was drenched, dripping water everywhere.

Blake returned with a stack of more towels, closing the lid to the toilet before placing the pile there.

While she dried Corky, Blake used a towel to dry Erika's hair, patting it against her head before wrapping it around the strands and slowly pulling it down to soak up the water.

"Don't ever do that to me again, Corky," she whispered,

bending forward to place a million kisses on the dog's head. "I can't live without you," Erika murmured, smiling through the tears when Corky rubbed her damp face against Erika's cheek. "You're my everything."

She was amazed by how she'd lost her heart to the sweet creature in such a short time. Two months in and Corky completely owned her.

Blake reached around Erika, petting Corky as well. "You listen to her, Cork, because I'm pretty sure I just lost ten years off my life."

Erika bowed her head, consumed with guilt. "I'm so sorry."

"What?" Blake grabbed her shoulders, twisting her to face him. "What do you mean you're sorry?"

"I lost her. She could have been hit by a car or…" Erika couldn't recall the last time she'd cried this much, but there was no holding back the tears tonight.

Everything that had been stressing her out finally caught up to her, and between the storm, her guilty feelings about Doug, her overwhelming attraction to Blake, and nearly losing Corky, she was an emotional mess right now.

"Don't you dare apologize, Erik. And if you're blaming yourself, stop right now. She broke free of the leash. That wasn't your fault."

Erika couldn't accept that. "I must not have hooked it completely." She pushed several wet strands of hair away from her face. "And I know she hates storms. I should have waited for it to pass before taking her outside. I thought we could get our walk in before it started. I was so stupid and—"

"Stop talking." Blake cupped her face, tilting her head back. "Repeat after me. We found Corky. She's fine."

Erika bit her lower lip when it started to tremble.

"Say it, Erik."

"We found Corky. She's fine," she whispered.

"Say it again," he demanded.

"We found her. She's fine."

Blake made her repeat those same words three more times.

"There. Believe it now?" he asked.

She nodded. "We found her and she's fine." This time, those two truths sank deep and consoled her.

"Good." Blake reached for Corky, who was now dry, and placed her on the floor, the two of them watching as she scampered out of the bathroom. Erika could hear her tiny paws clicking across the kitchen tiles, no doubt hungry after her grand adventure.

"Oh, to be a dog," she muttered. "And have that short a memory. By the way, I'm taking her to the vet tomorrow and getting her chipped."

Blake smiled, but it was a weak one, concern still in his gaze. She couldn't blame him. She wasn't the type to fall apart, and tonight she'd done so in spectacular fashion.

She didn't have to look in the mirror to know her eyes were puffy from crying, which meant, her face was probably bright red and blotchy. She was the ugliest crier on the planet.

"Okay. Your turn." Blake tugged her soaked jacket off and dropped it onto the floor.

"My turn for what?"

Blake didn't respond. Instead, he reached for the hem of her sweater and pulled it over her head with one squishy tug, dumping it with the jacket, leaving her in her bra.

Erika's arms flew to cover herself.

"Blake—" she started.

"Be a good girl and stand still," he said in that same deep, sexy voice that had taught her how to pleasure herself. "I'm going to take care of you."

CHAPTER EIGHT

BLAKE HELD his breath for a split second, part of him expecting her to pull away. He hoped that didn't happen because her anguish, her almost tangible fear, had shaken him to the core, and he needed to take care of her as much as she needed someone to console her.

Erika blinked slowly, her gaze locked on his. He could see her trying to process his intentions. He was used to his Erik being confident, steady, low-key, and positive.

None of those things were present at the moment.

While her shaking had stopped, every now and then, another tear slid down her cheek. He wasn't sure she realized she was still crying.

"I…" she whispered, pausing, then—hallelujah—nodding.

"Stay right there." He placed a kiss on her cheek.

Heading to his bedroom, he quickly rummaged through his dresser drawers for clothing for her. Crossing the hall to grab some of her own things felt like too big a journey to make. He didn't want to leave her alone long enough for Erika to come up with an excuse to leave.

Returning to the bathroom, he was pleased—and surprised—

to discover her exactly as he'd left her. Numbness and exhaustion were winning the day in his poor girl.

Blake grabbed another towel, using it to dry off her arms, her back, and her chest. The fact her bra was as wet as her shirt told him she'd been out in the elements for way too long. He tugged the T-shirt he'd grabbed for her over her head, unsurprised that it hung to mid-thigh. He had at least six inches on Erika, and he had to size up to accommodate his muscular arms, so the extra-large shirt swallowed her runner's body.

He heard her sharp intake of breath when he reached beneath the shirt, his arms encircling her so that he could find the hooks on her bra. Once it was unfastened, he pulled his arms away and gave her a smile.

"Do that woman trick where you pull it off with the shirt on," he said.

She laughed lightly, the sound music to his ears after the pain of listening to his typically happy best friend sobbing.

She pulled the straps of her bra free of her arms beneath the shirt and deposited the bra on top of the growing pile of wet clothing.

Blake wasted no time moving on to the next part, worried this might be the bridge too far. Kneeling before her, he helped her out of her socks and shoes. Then he lifted the hem of the shirt just enough that he could reach the button and zipper on her jeans. The wet denim was clinging to her legs, which meant, he had his work cut out for him in terms of stripping it off.

Erika remained still when he unfastened the jeans, then she tried to help, shimmying her hips as he worked the tight denim down. It took a couple of minutes before they managed to get the jeans completely off.

Rising, he bent slightly, reaching for the elastic of her panties. For the first time, Erika showed some resistance, her hands gripping his wrists to stop him.

"They're wet too," he murmured, his lips close to her ear. "I have some clean boxers for you to put on."

He expected her to insist on returning to her place for clothes, so he was surprised when, instead, she slowly released his wrists, allowing him to continue.

Pulling the panties down, he encouraged her to kick them off before he knelt once more, helping her into the boxer briefs. He tried to be a gentleman, tried not to look at her, but he failed.

That was when he admitted he hadn't really tried at all.

His teammates' comment that she was his girlfriend kept pinging around in his brain, and with each passing minute, the truth of that statement became more and more obvious.

Now that he'd opened his eyes to it, it was glaringly obvious.

Unfortunately, Erika was either as oblivious as he'd been, or she didn't view him in that way. After all, she'd been on a date tonight with Doug…the tool. He realized just how immature and jealous his feelings toward the other man were. Especially considering he'd only met the asshole once and he had seemed *nice*.

Not that it mattered.

Doug was trying to steal Blake's…girlfriend.

Fuck it. He wasn't going to pretend she wasn't that anymore, wasn't going to keep using the wrong signifiers. She wasn't his neighbor or his best friend. Or at least, she wasn't *just* those things.

No. First and foremost, she was his girlfriend. But given the hellish night she'd had, he knew tonight wasn't the night to drop that bomb on her.

Once she was changed, Blake led her into his bedroom. Pulling back the duvet, he pointed at the mattress. "Lie down."

Erika's brows furrowed, but he refused to give her a chance to argue.

"Your skin is still cool and clammy. You need to get warm or you'll get sick. Besides," he added, "I'm not letting you go home until we talk about what happened tonight."

Erika sighed. "I don't suppose we could just chalk it up to a bad night and forget about it."

He crossed his arms. "What do you think?"

The fact that she gave in, lying down on the bed without making a fuss, told him just how beaten down Erika was.

Returning to his dresser, Blake pulled out a pair of lounge pants for himself. He stepped into the bathroom to change, not willing to press his luck with her. She was in his bed, where she belonged, and he intended to see that she stayed there.

He didn't bother with a shirt. He probably should have grabbed one, but it wasn't like Erika hadn't seen him shirtless countless times before. The idea of building on the intimacy between them appealed to him. And even though he had no intention of doing anything more than talking to her tonight, he wanted her to become comfortable with him in his bed.

"Stay there." He headed toward the door that led to the hallway. "I want to lock up and check on Corky."

Once again, he worked fast, locking the door to his apartment, then checking Corky's bowls. She had plenty of food and water. She'd sacked out on the couch, lifting her head when he entered the living room. When he started back toward the bedroom, he grinned when he heard her little feet tapping on the floor behind him. On nights when she was with him, she always slept in his bed. She was a very affectionate dog, which meant, she didn't sleep on her half of the bed but on *his* side, with him. If he rolled away in the middle of the night, Corky would shift so that some part of her body was snuggled next to him. It was adorable.

Blake turned off the hall light when he entered the bedroom. Because of the cloudy skies, there was very little light provided from outside, so he crossed to the bathroom, turning that light on before closing the door, leaving it open just a few inches. He wanted to be able to see Erika's face as they talked, wanted to read her emotions and comfort her if she started to cry again.

He crossed to his side of the bed, crawling beneath the covers. If Erika was surprised by that, she didn't reveal it. Blake lay down next to her, facing her. The two of them chuckled softly when Corky hopped on the bed, prancing right between them, settling down in the middle.

Within seconds, the sweet puppy had closed her eyes and fallen sound asleep. Blake figured it wouldn't be long before she started snoring softly.

Erika lay on her back, hugging the edge of her side of the bed. Despite the fact she was obviously tired, her eyes were wide open, starting at the ceiling.

"Roll over, Erik. Look at me."

She did as he said, her sad eyes focused on him.

Reaching out, he brushed a strand of hair away from her face, then cupped her cheek. "Are you okay?"

She started to nod, then changed her response to a one-shoulder shrug.

"What happened?"

Erika blew out a slow breath, her response seemingly coming from left field. "Did I ever tell you why I became a doctor?"

He frowned, confused, then shook his head. "No. You didn't."

Erika bit her lip. "When I was younger, I was a bit of a wild child."

He grinned. "You're going to have to define wild child, because I'm having trouble picturing you in my version of that term."

"I sort of broke bad when I started high school. I'm an only child, and my parents were pretty overprotective."

Blake had spent a fair amount of time with Mr. and Mrs. Nelson, the older couple always very welcoming and kind. He attributed Erika's easygoing nature to them because they struck him as the type of people to go with the flow. "Guess them being overprotective makes sense. My mom had to spread her protectiveness a bit thinner, considering she was raising me, my needy-ass half-brother, and my two crazy stepbrothers."

Erika smiled, perfectly aware that Blake adored all three of his younger siblings. His mom had married Alan, his stepdad, when Blake was eight. Alan, who had full custody of his boys from his previous marriage, brought Marco and Todd—six and seven, respectively—into Blake's family. A couple of years after Alan and Mom married, they had Julian. The baby of the family, Julian had probably been the most doted-on kid in the world because in addition to Mom and Alan, he'd managed to wrap his three big brothers around his finger as well.

"Your brothers are awesome."

He pretended to disagree. "Glad you think so. I'm willing to sell them to you. Super cheap."

She reached out, shoving at his shoulder lightly. "Be careful because I might take you up on that offer. I've always wanted siblings."

Blake realized they'd strayed off topic. "You were about to tell me about your wild-child days."

Erika grimaced. "When I started high school, I hooked in with a not-great group of friends. One of the girls, Melanie, came from a home where there wasn't a lot of supervision, so we hung out in her basement a lot, sneaking her dad's beer, her mom's cigarettes, and taking hits from her older brother's bong."

Blake's eyebrows rose. "No way." While Erika liked her wine, he never would have imagined she'd been a smoker—of cigarettes *or* pot.

"I'm not proud of the way I behaved back then. I'd always been an honor roll student in elementary and middle school, but that did not hold true for the first semester of ninth grade. My report card was a potpourri of C's, D's, and even an F in English. I hate creative writing."

That part didn't surprise him at all. While he enjoyed reading fiction—he was a big fan of mysteries—Erika's chosen "pleasure" reading was the nonfiction variety, shit that would bore Blake to tears.

"Melanie's neighbor, Troy, started coming over a lot while we were hanging. He was seventeen and a junior—he'd been held back one year. He had his own car and a tattoo of a snake on his arm, and I thought he was the epitome of cool," Erika continued. "We started dating, and his best friend, Jacob, started going out with Melanie, so our basement hijinks evolved into massive make-out sessions. Until my report card arrived."

"Grounded?" Blake asked.

She nodded. "Big-time. On the heels of that, my mom found out about Troy and put her foot down on us dating, claiming no good would come from a seventeen-year-old boy going out with a fourteen-year-old girl. I cried and yelled and told them they were ruining my life…typical teenage girl stuff. But they didn't relent. Being kept away from my true love was the worst form of torture," she said sarcastically, "so when Troy texted one night, telling me to sneak out, I agreed. I thought I was in love…and I'd decided he should be my first."

While Blake knew the story was ancient history, he was having a hard time not wanting to track down Troy and beat the shit out of him. "So you snuck out?"

"Yeah. Crawled out my bedroom window and met Troy at the end of my block, where he was parked. He knew about some out-of-the-way country road right outside the city where we could park…and other things."

Erika slowly stroked her hand along Corky's back as she told the story. Her eyes had a faraway look, and he could imagine her replaying that night in her mind.

"We'd just hit the city limits when the storm started. It was a really nasty one. The weather forecasters had been warning about flash flooding. Troy's country road was narrow with lots of sharp turns. He was driving too fast, and I told him so, but he just laughed and teased me about being scared."

Blake had a feeling where this story was headed.

"On one bad turn, he ran off the road. There was a sharp incline, and given the speed he was driving, we had enough momentum that the car flipped over into a ditch. It probably would have flipped over a few times, but we were stopped by a tree on the driver's side. Troy's side."

"Jesus."

There was enough light in the room for him to see that Erika had gone pale, the memory bad enough to still provoke fear. He reached across Corky, placing his hand on her waist. He gave it a gentle squeeze. "You don't have to talk about it if—"

"No," she interjected. "I've actually never talked about that night, never told *anyone*… I've always been too ashamed of my actions. But I want to tell you."

Blake wasn't sure what to make of that, but he was more than capable of shouldering as much of this weight as he could if she was willing to share the load with him.

"The roof of the car sank into the ditch, which was deep with water from the thunderstorm. It was still raining, a total deluge —just like tonight. It was pitch black except for the occasional strikes of lightning. When one flashed, I was able to see that Troy was unconscious and bleeding a lot. I tried to unfasten my seat belt, but it was stuck. And even if I'd managed, the roof of the car had crushed in enough that there was no way I could get the car door open or crawl out of the window."

Blake shifted, wanting to get closer to Erika. His movement woke Corky, who took exception to being smushed between them. She stood, stretching dramatically before moving to the foot of the bed to sleep there. Blake quickly filled the space she'd just vacated, turning to lay on his back while wrapping his arm around Erika's shoulders, pulling her close enough that she could use his bare chest as a pillow.

"I know you're here and you're obviously okay, but, Erik, I need you to get to the end of this story quicker because I'm stressing the fuck out right now."

She gave him a breathy laugh that was less humor, more an attempt to mask a sob.

He tightened his grip.

"I kept calling out Troy's name, but he never answered. I started to worry that maybe he was dead, and panic set in, hard.

We were upside down in a ditch, with the rain pounding outside. I kept imagining the water was rising and I was terrified I'd drown. A couple of cars passed, but I guess they couldn't see us."

"I can't even imagine how scared you must have been."

"It was bad," she admitted. "So I did what most people in life or death situations do. I started making deals with fate, God, Buddha, whoever I thought might be listening, promising to change my ways. I swore I'd be a good daughter, that I'd get good grades, and that I'd dedicate my life to saving others if only I could live."

"Erik," Blake said softly, tilting her face so that she was looking at him. He was moved by her story and her commitment. She'd made a deal with some unseen force, and she kept her promise. It was all just so…her. "You stuck by your vow."

"I had to. Because after an hour or so, someone drove by, and they *did* see us. They called 9-1-1, and soon we were surrounded by first responders. Even with help there, we were still trapped and the water was rising. The firefighters had to use the jaws of life to cut us out of the car." She stopped, taking several labored breaths.

Blake placed a kiss on the side of her head. "I understand now why you're so afraid of thunderstorms."

"And tight spaces," she added. "My claustrophobia is no joke."

"What happened after they got you out of the car?"

"We were transported to the hospital."

"Troy was alive?" he asked.

She nodded. "Yes, but he spent a couple of nights in ICU. Broke his arm in three places and his femur."

Blake winced.

"He also hit his head hard and there was swelling of the brain."

"What about you?" Blake asked.

"I was very lucky. I had a minor concussion and hellacious

bruising, especially on my chest and shoulder from the seat belt, but I was treated and released that night."

"Your parents must have been out of their minds," he observed.

Erika went quiet for a moment, nodding slowly. "I heard my mom talking to one of the cops in the ER. She said they didn't even realize I wasn't in my room."

Blake recalled the night Erika told him about Sara dying, about her mother saying the same thing. He was beginning to understand why Sara's passing had hit her so hard.

Blake stroked her hair. "Were they angry?"

"Honestly? No. My mom did her usual protective momma bear thing, getting a list of dos and don'ts from the nurses and doctors in terms of how to take care of me…while my dad didn't say a word. He just stepped next to the hospital bed and pulled me into his arms, hugging me for the longest time, while I cried and apologized and promised I would never disobey them again."

"Given the fact you're a doctor, I'd say you turned over a new leaf."

She lifted her head. "I walked away from the bad-influence friends, broke up with Troy, got straight A's every semester after that, and started taking the path that would lead me to medical school."

"You're amazing."

Erika narrowed her eyes and shook her head. "No. I'm not. I made a bad decision, and I almost paid for it with my life. I thought I'd turned things around, and I was okay with what had happened that night, but then…" She swallowed heavily. "Sara." Her voice broke on the other girl's name.

Blake understood. "She didn't get the chance to turn things around."

Quiet tears slid down Erika's cheeks. "She fell for the wrong boy and made one stupid split-second decision—just like I did when I got into Troy's car. I can't understand why she died when I lived."

"Life doesn't play fair, Erik. It's a roll of the dice."

She obviously didn't like that answer.

"I kept picturing my parents' faces, getting the same news about me that I had to deliver about Sara. I…" She sighed. "I don't know. I think I've spent the last couple of weeks dealing with survivor's guilt."

Blake could understand that. "That makes sense in a way."

"It's been on my mind a lot, so when that storm hit tonight and Corky broke the leash and ran… Too much bad shit came up, and I lost it. I'm sorry about that, by the way."

He cupped her face, forcing her to look at him again. "I already told you I didn't want to hear you apologize. You have nothing to be sorry about." He kissed her forehead, then her cheek, then gave her a soft kiss on the lips.

Erika didn't hesitate to kiss him back, which felt like progress.

When they pulled apart, she smiled, one that was devoid of the same lingering sadness he'd seen in her expression all night.

"Thank you for telling me that story."

"Thank you for listening. I don't know why I never told you before. I guess…even after all these years, I'm still ashamed of my behavior."

Blake grinned. "You were fourteen years old. That's when we all do stupid shit designed to make our parents crazy."

He felt some of the tension leave her body. "Bet you gave your mom a run for her money."

"You know I did," he said, his tone pure bragging. He spent the next ten minutes filling her in on his teenage exploits, his stories cracking her up as she finally turned the corner on her fears and anguish for good.

"You know," Erika said. "You've never told me why you decided to pursue hockey."

"Oh, that's an easy one. Because of my stepdad."

She looked at him, clearly waiting for him to expound.

"That's it? Not much of a storyteller, are you?" she teased.

Blake grinned. "You know my dad split when I was three." He and Erika had discussed childhoods near the beginning of their friendship, so she knew his dad had an affair with a coworker and decided to dump family number one to start family number two. Maybe Blake would have been bitter about that if he hadn't had the world's greatest mom and stepdad. Mom had never let him feel the absence of his dad, taking on both roles with ease. When he told her he wanted to play hockey—because his best friend in second grade did—she signed him up, bought the equipment, and started watching the sport in an attempt to understand it.

"I know about your dad leaving," Erika confirmed.

"When I started playing hockey, Alan was my first coach. That's how he and my mom met. He knew she was a single mom with very little knowledge of the sport, so he spent extra time helping me, teaching me the basics along with Todd, who was also on the team. I was hooked on the sport from day one, and Alan was my biggest cheerleader. He said he knew right from the start that I had the talent to play professionally. He encouraged me without pushing, always patiently guiding without putting any pressure on me, if that makes sense. I still go to him if I find myself struggling with some part of my game. I've had countless hockey coaches in my life, but he's been the best."

"I've always liked Alan," Erika confessed, "but now, I think I love him. I'm so glad you had him in your life."

"Me too. Because I'm sure that without him, I wouldn't be where I am today. He set me on the path to the best life ever."

Erika smiled. "So cool."

Then Blake said something he'd never admitted aloud. "I hope I can be as good a father to my kids as he was to me and my brothers."

"Kids?" Erika tilted her head. "I'm not sure I've ever heard you say you want kids."

He gave her a serious look. "Of course I do." What he didn't add was that he wanted them with *her*, wanted to see her belly grow round as she carried his son or daughter. God willing, they'd have one of each.

She raised one eyebrow. "Well, you might want to reconsider your timeframe for acquiring a ball and chain, otherwise people are going to think you're the grandfather when you go to all the school functions."

Blake ruffled her hair playfully. "I'll take that under advisement."

Erika covered her mouth with her hand, trying to hide a yawn. "I should probably go home."

He shook his head. "Nope. We're having a sleepover."

"Aren't we a little old for slumber parties?"

Blake chuckled. "Never too old." He leaned closer and gave her another kiss on the head. He wanted to expand on it, wanted to kiss her and hold her and take her the way he'd spent too many nights fantasizing about…ever since that masturbation lesson.

Erika didn't put up a fight—mercifully. Instead, she nestled into his arms, resting her cheek on his chest and closing her eyes.

Five minutes hadn't passed before he recognized the deep, even breathing that told him she'd fallen asleep. Not that he was surprised after the night she'd had.

Sleep took longer for Blake. Not because he was stressed out or anxious but because he wanted to savor the feeling of Erika in his arms.

Having her here in his bed, Corky asleep at their feet…

He sighed, aware that his world had just clicked into place.

Everything in this moment was exactly how it was supposed to be.

Now he just had to find a way to keep it.

CHAPTER NINE

ERIKA OPENED HER EYES SLOWLY, blinking a few times. She knew exactly where she was, as she'd stirred a couple times during the night. She'd never woken up, exactly, but she'd felt Blake shift in the bed, the two of them doing a bit of choreography in terms of comfortable sleep positions. She had been cognizant enough to think, "I should go home," but drowsy enough to fall back to sleep immediately.

Right now, she was the little spoon to Blake's big one. His muscular arm was wrapped around her waist—her *bare* waist, as the huge T-shirt he'd loaned her last night had ridden up, bunched just under her breasts. His boxer briefs had traveled a different direction, hanging low on her ass. She was surprised they'd stayed on at all, given how loose they were on her.

Blake was breathing heavily behind her, sleeping deeply.

She was glad because it gave her time to figure out her next move.

Last night had been one fuck-up after another, starting with her failed date with Doug, her panic attack in the midst of the storm, and losing Corky. God, she really hated crying in front of people, especially over something as stupid as a phobia. Erika prided herself on being able to control her fear of thunder and lightning. Until last night, no one had ever discovered her secret terror.

The one thing that hadn't felt like a mistake, even though it really should, was sleeping with Blake. Probably because nothing happened between them that was truly out of the norm.

Except the part where she fell apart. She was usually able to hold her shit together better.

Blake, however, had done what he always did. Took care of her. Comforted her. Listened to her. Found a way to make her laugh.

Those were normal, familiar things. The only part that was different was the fact they were in stages of undress and lying in his bed rather than fully clothed and sitting in his living room or hanging out in her kitchen.

He hadn't tried to kiss her…not really. Hadn't made what was happening between them sexual. His actions had been friendly and painfully platonic.

Although…

Erika shifted the tiniest bit, pressing her ass backward until—

Yep. Blake had a hard-on.

Not that she should read anything into that. A lot of guys woke up with erections. It probably didn't help that she was cuddled against him. Blake was no stranger to sleepovers, so he was probably blissfully lost in some dream state, mistaking her for one of his puck bunnies.

That idea was a sobering one.

Glancing at the clock on the nightstand, she was surprised to discover it was a little past nine a.m. She *never* slept late. An early riser, she'd usually finished her five-mile run, showered, and eaten her yogurt by this time of day.

Erika glanced over her shoulder, smiling as she took in Blake's rumpled hair, his five-o'clock shadow, the crease on his cheek left from a wrinkle in the pillowcase. He was a gorgeous man. She'd have to be dead not to notice that, but ordinarily she was able to look past—or maybe *ignore* was a better word—that fact to focus on their friendship.

Right now, all her girlie bits were awake and drooling over the hot guy spooning her.

Erika looked away and closed her eyes.

Stop.

Nothing had changed between them last night. Blake had offered her an ear and a shoulder; shown her the same friendship he'd been offering for the better part of three years.

Time to regroup.

Erika slowly lifted Blake's arm, moving it off her in centimeters, careful not to wake him. It took her a full five minutes to extract herself from his embrace, and luckily, he remained asleep throughout.

Corky was still sacked out at the foot of the bed. She lifted her head when Erika rose from the bed, yawning widely. Then the lazy pup put her head down and went back to sleep.

Erika was grateful. If Corky had started whining to go out, her escape would have been foiled. Tiptoeing to the bathroom, she bent to retrieve her clothing. She didn't bother changing because most of what she was wearing last night was still damp, and it wasn't like she had far to go.

She dug into the pocket of her jeans for her key, then quietly headed through the apartment. She knew Blake would be over as soon as he woke up, but she was hoping to have showered and dressed and girded her loins before that happened.

Opening the door, she stepped into the hallway—

Stopping short when she spotted Doug standing outside her place.

He'd been about to knock, but he turned when he heard Blake's door open.

"Erika?" He was frowning, his gaze traveling from head to foot. He obviously put two and two together and came up with sex, as his frown darkened to a scowl.

"What are you doing here?" she asked.

There were two different voices at war in her head when it came to Doug. There was one that felt guilty for allowing him to think the two of them were embarking on something real when her feelings had been so shaky. Then there was the one that was pissed about the true colors he'd shown last night, when she hadn't invited him in. There was no rule book that said a woman had to have sex with a man after a certain number of dates. If she wasn't ready, then she wasn't fucking ready. Period.

The guilty side wanted to tell him this wasn't what it looked like, while the annoyed side wanted to tell him what she did was none of his damn business.

She closed the door to Blake's apartment quietly, wishing she wasn't doing such an amazing impersonation of the walk of shame.

Doug lifted the bag and cup holder in his hands. "I felt bad about the way things ended last night. I wanted to apologize over coffee and donuts."

Shit.

"How did you…" she started, wondering how he'd gotten into the building.

He anticipated her question. "One of your neighbors was leaving as I got here."

She unlocked her door, gesturing for him to come in with a tilt of her head. He was clearly pissed, so this wasn't going to be an easy conversation, but she owed it to him to break things off the right way.

He followed her in, setting the coffee and donuts on the island counter, while she deposited her damp clothes in the laundry area, dumping them in the washing machine without turning it on. She'd deal with them later.

Returning to the kitchen, she kept the island between them, trying to shield herself from his view. She glanced down at her attire and sighed, realizing he'd already gotten an eyeful. "This isn't what it looks like."

Doug barked out an angry laugh. "Yeah, right."

"I lost Corky last night in the storm. Blake helped me find her. We brought her inside, changed into dry clothes, and fell asleep."

"Your clothes and bed are right here. Why did you need *his*?"

Erika wasn't sure how to answer that.

No, she didn't want to because it really *wasn't* any of his business.

If she'd still been on the fence about any sort of future with Doug before, it was clear she had hurdled it. Not only was she not attracted to him, she wasn't even sure she liked him that much. It felt as if she'd been trying to turn him into Mr. Right because she was lonely, and her brain kept telling her they were a good match.

She walked around the counter to stand in front of him, grateful he hadn't closed the door behind him because she intended to herd him toward it as she spoke. "Doug, this isn't working."

He scoffed derisively. "No shit."

Erika didn't like his tone or his words, but she refused to lose her temper. Getting emotional would only make this harder. "I don't think we should see each other anymore."

"Guess me stopping by unannounced fucked with your plan."

"What?" she asked, confused. "What plan?"

Doug crossed his arms. "You had the best of both worlds. Had me wining and dining you before coming home to fuck Mr. Hockey Stud."

Erika narrowed her eyes. Fuck staying calm. "Wining and dining me? You realize I paid for half those dates." She'd insisted they take turns because she didn't subscribe to the old-fashioned idea that the man should pay. "I think you should leave. *Now.*" She raised her voice on the last word, but her anger didn't appear to penetrate, as Doug's was burning hotter.

"You think it was funny? Making me look like a fucking fool, acting like you were some sweet, innocent woman looking for true love when the truth is you're nothing but a slut?"

"Get. Out!" she yelled.

"Fuck you!" Doug yelled back.

Erika could only assume it spoke to her blessed life that she never saw what was coming next.

Flames lit the side of her face as Doug backhanded her so hard, she stumbled and nearly fell. The only thing that stopped her was Doug himself. He grabbed her upper arms, holding her tight, shaking her violently.

"You fucking bitch!"

Erika struggled hard, trying to break free of his grip. "Let go! *Let go!*"

Her teeth rattled as he shook her harder—and she realized she was in big trouble.

Then she was shocked when suddenly, Doug released her. That surprise only lasted a split second when a blur flew past her. Erika blinked a few times, her mind trying to make sense of what she was seeing.

Blake had Doug by the throat, pinned against the far wall.

"What the fuck are you doing?" Blake's dark tone was pure murder.

Doug snarled, even as he tried to pry Blake's fingers off. "Fuck you!"

Blake didn't relent. Instead, he used his iron-like grip to pull Doug away from the wall, dragging him toward the door.

Doug wasn't fighting too hard, no doubt spying the exit. "Let me go, you prick!"

"If you ever come around here again, if you ever lay your hands on her again—" Blake seethed as he pushed Doug toward the door.

"You can have her," Doug spat. "I'm not interested in a cock tease or a fucking slut!"

One second, Doug was standing; the next, he was on the

floor, blood pouring from his nose as Blake hovered over him, fists clenched by his side.

Doug crab-crawled backward when it looked like Blake was going to pick him up and ring the bell on round two. As he cleared the doorway after crawling into the hall, Doug rose, his eyes darting over to the stairwell as he swiped the back of his hand under his nose, smearing the blood on his cheek.

"Get the fuck out of here!" Blake took two steps forward, his fist rising again when Doug didn't leave immediately, but Erika moved faster, placing herself in front of him, her hands on his chest to hold him back.

"It's over," she said, hoping her words would penetrate. She'd never seen her mild-mannered best friend so angry. His gaze was still locked on Doug, and it was obvious Blake wasn't finished yet.

Glancing over her shoulder, Erika realized she was close enough to kick the door closed with her foot. So she did, slamming it loudly.

The noise finally broke through the white-hot haze that seemed to surround Blake. His shoulders were still tight, but he unclenched fists and for the first time since entering her apartment, he looked at her.

And the anger returned tenfold.

"Did he *hit* you?" His finger gently tipped her chin up, the soft touch in direct counterpoint to the pure venom in his voice.

"I'm okay."

"That wasn't what I asked," Blake said through gritted teeth.

"He's gone. It's over."

Blake didn't look like he agreed with that assessment. "He fucking hit you," he muttered. "He put his hands on you. I should've hit him harder. Should have hit him again."

She shook her head, forcing her lips to make what she hoped would pass for a smile. "You hit him plenty hard. I think you broke his nose."

Blake rubbed his knuckles. They were red from the punch

and one had split, a tiny trickle of blood sliding down his middle finger.

"You're hurt." Erika grabbed his uninjured hand and tugged him toward the kitchen sink. Reaching for a paper towel, she wet it, gently patting at the small cut.

"Are you fucking kidding me?" Blake pulled his hand away from hers, cupping her jaw, turning her face. Her cheek still stung, so she had no doubt it was blood red. "I don't give a shit about my hand. Erika, that son of a bitch hit you!"

The fact he used her full name told her just how upset he was.

"It was just a little slap." She might have sold her lie better if her voice hadn't broken and her eyes clouded with tears.

Blake's anger faded in an instant, every drop of tension in his body finally melting when he tugged her into his warm, strong embrace. "Erik," he murmured, rubbing his hands up and down her back.

Last night, she'd fallen apart in front of him. She wasn't going to do that again, so she dug deep, shoving everything that had happened in the last ten minutes into a hole and covering it over.

Her dad had claimed once that she got her inner strength from his mother, able to tuck her emotions away until she was alone. Erika considered that, recalling the day her grandfather had died unexpectedly of a massive heart attack. Her parents, aunts, uncles, and cousins had been crying as they tried to make sense of the loss. Through it all, Grandma had consoled them, her eyes dry. Erika had been young enough to mistake her grandmother's response as a lack of caring, until Dad explained his mother would shed her tears later, alone, when they wouldn't add to the pain everyone else was already feeling. Erika had admired that attribute, and from that day on, she aspired to be like her grandmother.

Somehow, she managed to regain control quickly, pulling away from Blake's hug, proud her eyes were dry.

He studied her face closely. It was obvious he expected her to be upset. "I hate that he hit you. That I wasn't here to stop him."

"It's not your job to protect me."

"The fuck it's not," Blake countered hotly.

Erika didn't bother to protest because, while she was on steadier ground, he was still under the influence of a fuck-ton of adrenaline. Blake had gotten one swing in, but she suspected it hadn't satisfied his instinct to defend. She'd seen him do the same on the ice whenever he felt one of his teammates had been wronged by an opponent. He was no stranger to a guns-blazing approach to perceived slights.

"You came when I needed you." She hoped it would be enough to soothe that part of him that was no doubt kicking himself for something that wasn't his fault.

"What the hell happened?"

She'd anticipated the question because she hadn't told Blake about her wavering feelings toward Doug. As far as he knew, she liked the man and had been working on building a relationship with him.

"Losing Corky wasn't my only fuck-up last night. Doug's been hinting at wanting a physical relationship, but I kept putting him off."

"Why?"

It was a fair question.

"I wasn't attracted to him...sexually," she added, though she didn't need to.

"Then why did you keep going out with him?"

She sighed. "That was the fuck-up part. I kept telling myself I wasn't giving him a fair shake, that maybe those feelings would grow. Until today—or actually, last night—I thought he was a really nice guy."

Blake scowled. "What happened last night?"

"We went to dinner and the movies, and then he drove me home. I think he was expecting an invitation to come inside. I...I couldn't do it. He lost his temper—"

Blake growled, and she put her hands up quickly.

"Not like today. He asked if we were ever going to fuck. Just like that. Sort of aggressive and rude. I was annoyed by his tone. Told him I wouldn't be rushed into sex, and he left in a huff." Erika gestured toward the coffee and uneaten bag of donuts. "He came by this morning to apologize. Unfortunately, I was coming out of your apartment…" She looked down at her clothes—or rather, Blake's. "He obviously jumped to the conclusion that I'd rejected him, then came upstairs and crawled into bed with you."

"None of that gave him the right to hit you," Blake said hotly.

"I agree one-hundred percent. I never would have expected…" She swallowed heavily. "No one's ever hit me before."

Blake reached out, pulling her back into his arms, though she wasn't sure if this hug was to comfort her or him. "I still want to hunt that guy down and teach him a fucking lesson."

"No. It's over."

"I don't understand what part of that was a fuck-up," he said.

"I should have broken things off with Doug sooner. Shouldn't have kept stringing him along." She shook her head, a lame attempt to basically shake all the bad thoughts from her head. "Anyway, it's over and done, and I don't want to talk about this anymore."

Blake opened his mouth, but she lifted her hand to halt whatever he might say.

"Ever," she stressed. "I don't want to talk about it ever."

Blake scowled, but mercifully, he kept his mouth closed.

"Thank you," she said, ready to put this morning's nightmare behind her. For the first time, they both noticed the sound of barking coming from Blake's apartment.

"Corky," they said at the same time.

"We were on our way over to see where you'd gone. When I heard the shouting, I shut her in my apartment," Blake explained.

It was past time for the puppy's potty break. A nice long walk and some fresh air was just what she needed.

"Oh." Erika glanced down at herself. "Give me a minute to change and I'll take her for a walk."

"I'll go with you," Blake said. "I'll run over and get her."

"You don't have to," Erika said. "I'm fine doing it alone."

Blake placed a hand on her shoulder, halting her when she started to walk by him. He'd donned a hoodie, jeans, and tennis shoes before coming over to find her. "I just kicked an abusive asshole out of here with a bloody nose and a chip on his shoulder. I want to make sure he left the area and isn't still hanging around. So, I'll repeat—I. Am. Going. With. You."

Erika hadn't considered that. She didn't think Doug would stick around on the off chance he ran into Blake again, but she also hadn't suspected he was a violent person either.

"Okay. It won't take me a second to change."

Blake headed for the door. "Take your time."

Erika threw on jeans and a heavy sweater, then pulled on thick socks and boots. Winter temperatures had arrived, and she recalled the weatherman warning that Baltimore would be lucky to get out of the teens today.

Blake and Corky were waiting for her in the hallway, the little dog prancing around impatiently.

"We better hurry," Blake said, "unless we want an accident."

Erika was surprised when Blake grabbed her hand with his free one, holding it like it was the most natural thing on earth. He was a tactile guy, always placing his hand on her back whenever they were walking on slippery surfaces, wrapping his arm around her shoulders when they were in a crowd, ruffling or playfully tugging her hair anytime she was being a smart-ass. He'd even played the gentleman when escorting her into that black-tie charity gala...but she couldn't remember him ever holding her hand like this.

It was nice.

Maybe too nice, because it was making that line she'd been so careful to draw between them, even fainter. Hell, at this point, it might be safer to say they'd erased the whole damn thing.

Erika shivered when they stepped outside into the frigid air. "Oh my God, it's cold."

Blake used his grip on her hand to pull her closer to him. "What's your plan for the day?"

"I have a couple of errands to run and I'm going to stop by the hospital for a little while. I have a patient I want to check on. Probably going to spend the rest of the day tackling a mountain of laundry and cleaning out my closet. It's sort of gotten away from me. You?"

"I have practice in a couple of hours."

"Hitting the pub with the guys after?" she asked.

Blake shook his head. "Nope. I'm coming home and you and I are going to have dinner together."

As wonderful as that sounded, Erika really did need to put up at least a token bit of resistance…if only to make herself feel as if she wasn't completely weak where Blake was concerned. "I don't think I'd be very good company tonight. You'd probably be better hanging with Tank."

Blake gave her a pointed look. "That's not going to happen."

"Why not?"

"Because contrary to what you think, we're not done talking about last night and this morning."

"Blake—" she started, way too weary to rehash any part of the past twelve hours.

"I didn't like waking up alone this morning, Erik. Why did you sneak out?"

She knew her escape wouldn't go unnoticed or uncommented on, but she'd been banking on having time to get her thoughts in order during a hot shower. She did her best thinking under the jets.

"I didn't sneak out," she argued. "I was just getting on with my day. What reason would I have had for sticking around?"

Blake clearly didn't like her question, his jaw clenching

slightly. Rather than respond with words, his answer came in the form of action.

He pulled her to him, his lips meeting hers in a kiss so incendiary, Erika forgot all about the cold.

This kiss was the least-friendly, least-platonic kiss in the history of kissing.

Erika raised her arms, wrapping them around his neck, feeling the need to hold on for dear life. My *God*, he could kiss.

As his lips literally devoured hers, his hands slipped beneath her jacket to caress her back, tickle her waist, fondle the sides of her breasts. Every touch felt less like an exploration and more like a claiming, and she was suddenly pissed at herself for putting on such a thick sweater.

What felt like hours later, he broke the kiss, placing his forehead against hers, grasping her hand and drawing it to the front placket of his jeans, letting her feel his very—VERY—erect dick tenting the front of his jeans. "I had a very good reason for you to stick around."

Erika didn't have a clue how to respond to that, so she didn't. Instead, she stared at him, wondering if she looked as shell-shocked as she felt.

"Come on. It's too cold out here." Blake turned them back in the direction of their building, neither of them speaking. When they reached their floor, Blake handed her Corky's leash. "I need to grab a quick shower. A cold one," he added with a wink. "Then head to practice. I'll meet you at your place for dinner around six."

She was shaking her head even before he finished speaking, even though nothing he'd said indicated that she was being given a choice. "Blake, I really don't think—"

"Good," he interrupted. "Keep on not thinking, because we're having dinner together. We can order something from DoorDash. Your choice."

Erika intended to continue the argument, but Blake was too

quick—or maybe determined was the better word. "Really, Blake. I—"

He walked away and entered his apartment, closing the door behind him before she could finish.

"Stubborn man," she muttered, more to herself than Corky. Letting herself into her apartment, she leaned against the door, searching for something that no longer existed.

Her willpower.

Between the storm, losing Corky, and Doug's attack, she was out of steam. But more than that, she was tired of fighting against something she really, *really* wanted.

Blake had accused her of depriving herself for years.

But not tonight.

Tonight, she was going to ignore all those solid reasons for why she shouldn't sleep with the sexiest man she'd ever known.

Tonight, she was going to give herself what was certain to be an evening she would never forget.

Tonight, she was throwing all caution to the wind because she was tired and sad and so fucking lonely.

Then, come morning…

Well, she'd figure that out tomorrow.

CHAPTER TEN

BLAKE KNOCKED on Erika's door once before turning the knob to enter. As always, his own personal Walmart greeter was right there at the ready. Scooping Corky into his arms, he glanced around Erika's apartment.

"Erik?"

"Be out in a minute," she called from the bedroom.

Blake toed off his shoes, then traipsed over to the couch with Corky squirming in his arms. He found one of her chew toys, the two of them playing tug-of-war while the least fearsome dog he'd ever known gave him the most adorable growl. She shook her head violently, trying to get the toy. Twice he let go, letting her have it, chuckling every time she returned it to him, attempting to put it back in his hand so he would continue the game.

Blake considered everything that had happened today to lead him to this moment. He'd been disoriented upon waking this morning, but that feeling soon morphed to annoyance when he realized he was alone.

Erika had snuck out like a thief in the night. Not that he could blame her. He'd spent the evening comforting her—like a friend would—rather than telling her that his feelings for her had changed.

Well, changed was probably the wrong word. Once his teammates pointed out who she was to him, it had opened his eyes to the fact he'd been falling head over ass in love with the sexy doctor since the first day she'd moved in. Rather than open himself to the idea of pursuing a relationship with a wonderful, funny, intelligent woman, he'd accepted Erika's decision that they couldn't be more than friends. Actually, he'd grabbed onto it like a lifeline to save his so-called blissful bachelor lifestyle.

He'd been an oblivious fool.

Pissed that she'd taken off this morning, Blake had thrown on some clothes, prepared to march over to her apartment to inform her that they had a new status quo.

Probably not his best plan.

God only knew how Erika would have reacted if he'd thrown open her door and stated point-blank that he was her boyfriend. She most likely would have laughed in his face, and she *should* have. But he hadn't just woken up alone. He'd woken up hard enough to drive nails into concrete, so there hadn't been enough blood in his brain for him to approach her with more finesse or tact.

Or, you know, any tact at all.

All thoughts of dragging her back to his bed vanished the second he'd heard yelling coming from her apartment.

Blake ran a hand through his hair, the same anger he'd felt this morning returning. He couldn't let himself think too hard about how badly Doug might have hurt her if he hadn't intervened. He'd met assholes like Doug before. Jealous guys with bad tempers and too much pride were bad fucking news.

He hated that Erika felt guilty, felt like she'd somehow led the jerk on.

"Sorry," Erika said as she entered the living room. "Did some laundry today…including putting clean sheets on the bed."

Blake enjoyed not only the way she blushed when she talked

about the clean sheets, but the fact she appeared to have done her hair and put on makeup. She was even wearing sexy skinny jeans and a pretty pink top with enough of a V-neck to give him the perfect peek of cleavage.

She was the queen of ponytails, lounge pants, and the natural look, so it wasn't often he saw her with her hair down, her eyes accentuated with liner and mascara. Erika was hands down the most beautiful woman he'd ever known, with or without trying…but damn if he wasn't pleased by her efforts tonight.

He'd worried a good bit today, concerned maybe he'd taken things too far, kissing her the way he had, letting her feel his hard-on. Blake had made it damn clear what he wanted to happen tonight, so he'd mentally prepared himself for her to kick up a fuss, to hit him with more of that "we're better off as friends" bullshit.

Now, it appeared all his anxious feelings had been for naught because not only was Erika not offering any resistance, it appeared she was all-in.

"What do you want for dinner?" He pulled his phone from the back pocket of his jeans.

She waved, indicating he could put it away. "Don't bother. I already ordered us a pizza. Hope that's okay."

He grinned. "Never met a pizza I wouldn't eat. Unless it's a Hawaiian one. Ham and pineapple on pizza is unnatural."

She laughed. "I've already tried and failed to convert you to those toppings several times. I've long ago accepted that you don't know what you're talking about when it comes to good pizza."

"Says the woman who won't eat buffalo chicken pizza," he countered.

"It's the buffalo, not the chicken." She made a face, her aversion to spicy foods well documented. "Unlike you, I cannot drink hot sauce from the bottle. It should be here—"

As if she'd summoned the pizza guy personally, the buzzer announcing she had company at the front entrance to the building went off. Erika crossed to the door. "Yes?" she said into the intercom.

"Pizza," the guy said.

She buzzed him in, then met him at her door, giving him a tip and thanking him.

Erika really had prepared for the night, carrying the pizza to the coffee table, drawing his attention to the paper plates and napkins she'd already set out.

"Beer or wine?" she asked.

"Whatever you're having."

She walked to the fridge, then returned to hand him a bottle of Stella. He popped the caps on both before tapping his against hers.

"To beer and pizza."

He laughed. "Amen."

Erika sat next to him on the couch as they reached in, grabbing steaming slices of pizza, thick with cheese and tomato sauce, pepperoni, and mushrooms. She'd ordered his favorite, and again, he felt like he'd been given an unexpected gift.

Nothing about tonight was going the way he'd anticipated. Not that he was upset about that at all.

"You doing okay?" He hated to remind her of this morning, but on top of worrying about how to get them from point A, the couch, to point B, the bedroom, he'd been stressed out about the shit Doug had put her through. He'd worked off quite a bit of pent-up aggression on the ice this afternoon, much to his teammates' dismay.

She nodded, and even gave him a genuine smile. "I am. My mother always said the best way to clear your head of negativity is to clean. So, on top of the laundry, I'm happy to say my closet has never looked better and there are currently six bags of clothes ready to be donated to charity."

"Damn. Very productive day."

"Yep. It was. And while I cleaned, I forced myself to face some painfully real facts."

Blake frowned. "Like what?"

"Like I am the worst judge of character when it comes to the guys I date."

Blake grimaced. "When it comes to Doug, I agree whole-heartedly. However, I wouldn't know about the rest. You're frustratingly tight-lipped when it comes to talking about your past relationships."

Erika rolled her eyes. "That's because I'm afraid you'll reciprocate, and I don't have eight hours to dedicate to listening to you go into detail about all your sexual escapades."

"You're only allotting eight hours for that?" he joked.

Erika snorted, then took a swig of her beer. "See? Ain't nobody got time for that."

Blake did a quick cross-his-heart motion. "I promise this doesn't have to be a tit-for-tat conversation. I'm just curious about this big bunch of duds you've apparently dated."

She giggled softly. "Not sure I'd call it a big bunch."

"How many exes are we talking about?"

Her smile faded into a grimace. "Two exes and one oopsie."

Blake tried to hold back his astonishment, but he failed miserably, his eyes widening. Erika was a gorgeous, intelligent, fun woman. How in the hell had she made it all the way to thirty with just three lovers? "You've only slept with three men?"

"Yup." She raised one hand, wiggling her fingers adorably. "Haven't even used all the fingers."

It was on the tip of his tongue to let her know she was *never* going to fill a one-handed quota, since her count was ending with him.

He was going to be Mr. Number Four and that was where her count was ending.

Still, Blake shook his head in disbelief.

"Don't look at me like that." Erika narrowed her eyes, though there was no heat behind her words or expression. "I told you when you were laying on the charm after I moved in…when I date, it's with an eye toward a committed relationship."

"So who were these three losers?" he asked, genuinely curious. "I already know you didn't lose your virginity to that prick Troy."

She grinned. "You have a bad habit of calling my exes names. Troy's a prick, Doug a tool. The rest are losers and duds?"

"If the shoe fits…" he grumbled. "FYI, Doug wasn't an ex. He was an asshole, and one who'd better hope he never runs into me again."

She reached over and placed a hand on his, giving it a quick squeeze. "Did I say thank you for this morning?"

"You don't have to thank me."

"Even so…" She leaned toward him, bumping her shoulder against his. "I do appreciate it."

"You're welcome. Now get to the good stuff." He waved his hand impatiently, aware she was stalling.

"Fine. I lost my virginity to the guy who was probably my first boyfriend. I'm not counting Troy because…well, I don't want to."

"I don't think he counts either."

"Reed and I lived in the same dorm our freshman and sophomore years of college. He was a…" Erika hesitated, and he realized why when she reluctantly finished, "Nice guy."

Blake chuckled. "Sounds to me like you have a type."

She huffed out a breath. "There's nothing wrong with being nice."

He didn't bother to pick at that argument because he didn't want to distract her from the conversation at hand. "So what happened with Reed?"

"He joined a fraternity toward the end of our sophomore year. Suddenly, it wasn't fun having study dates in the dorm room with your girlfriend when you could be getting wasted at the frat house. In the end, it turned out our goals for college were too different. He wanted to live the experience, while I wanted to earn a four-point-oh and get into medical school. He started partying all the time, and it ended when he found himself a bottle-blonde sorority girl named Amber, who he decided was more his type."

"Easy?"

His joke landed, and Erika smacked his arm as she laughed. "Totally."

"So who was the next boyfriend?" he asked.

"Charles. We met in medical school. We were friends the first couple of years, and then it turned into something more. We dated fairly steadily the last two years."

Blake was surprised he'd never heard her mention Charles before. "That's a long time to date someone, and the two of you were in your twenties—adults. You didn't think he was the one?"

"Actually, I did," she admitted. "But it turned out, he didn't. He was from an incredibly wealthy family in Boston. The type who live in legit mansions and spend their summers in Martha's Vineyard. I met his parents the second Christmas we were dating. It became obvious very quickly that they considered his relationship with me as Charles slumming it, especially when his mom introduced me to their neighbor's daughter, Sylvia—and I realized *exactly* who the folks were hoping he'd marry."

"Slumming? Seriously? You were studying to be a doctor. You're gorgeous, smart—"

"And the daughter of two lowly schoolteachers," she said, though he could tell she was trying to be funny. "Things were strained between us after that holiday. I thought it was because I was struggling to bring up the conversation about how his family didn't like me. Turns out, the *real* reason we weren't getting along was because he'd slept with Sylvia the night after I left Boston. I'd gone home to spend the rest of that holiday with my family."

"What a dick! Jesus."

"Yeah. I have to admit, that one hurt for a long time."

"So who was the third? The oopsie?" Blake asked, curious.

Her mouth twisted, and it was obvious she didn't want to

talk about number three. "Danny. I usually just refer to him as my moment of weakness. We were neighbors, both of us living in the same apartment building—the one I lived in prior to moving here. He was a good-looking guy and…"

"And?"

"I found out through a friend of a friend that Charles and Sylvia had gotten engaged a few months after I'd started my residency here. I was depressed and alone and out of wine, so I headed to a convenience store on the corner. I ran into Danny on the way back home. One thing led to another, and we split the wine and spent the night together.

"You know me and my silly brain. Sex isn't just a physical thing for me, so I stupidly thought what we'd shared was a genuine connection. The next morning, I was certain that we'd begin dating. Danny did *not* feel the same. I asked him out a few times before I finally got the message that he wasn't interested. So basically the seven months after that, until my lease ran out, was scattered with lots of awkward encounters whenever we ran into each other around the building."

And now Blake understood why Erika had been so dead set against going out with him.

She sighed. "I'm completely color blind, Blake, because I've never seen a red flag in my life. Both my long-term boyfriends cheated on me. I tried to make a one-night stand into a relationship, and me thinking that Doug was actually a nice guy just proves that time hasn't made me any smarter when it comes to romance and dating."

Blake wanted to tell her that *he* was the right guy, but then it occurred to him—they'd never been on a date. The second he had the thought, he found himself planning their first. He'd take her to The Capital Grille for a romantic dinner, then they could walk around Fell's Point and the Inner Harbor, holding hands, stealing kisses. The more he thought about it, the more he couldn't wait to make it a reality.

"So…at the risk of losing the next eight hours…do I want to

know your sexual partners number?" Erika asked, reminding him that this conversation was about past relationships, which felt very New Relationship 101 to him. Of course, Blake had never cared about any of the other women he'd slept with enough to ask about their dating history.

He tilted his head as if he didn't hear her question. "What?"

She repeated it, and he frowned.

"I can't hear you."

Erika asked again, while he pretended to clean out his ear.

"You really need to stop mumbling," he joked.

She laughed. "Fine. I've clearly gotten my answer, and you're right. I probably don't want to know."

"None of those women matter, Erik. The only one who matters is sitting in front of me. Here and now."

"Here and now," she repeated.

"I didn't like waking up alone this morning." He moved closer.

"So you said." Erika split the distance between them, her thigh pressed tightly against his.

"I notice you're not running for the hills." His face was close enough to hers that he could feel the heat from her breath.

"You're right," she said, moving so close that his cock went from half-mast to rock-hard in record time. "I'm not."

"Are you thinking about it?"

She shook her head. "Not even a little bit."

"Erik." His lips touched hers as he spoke.

"Hmm."

"Bedroom. Now."

Erika never missed a beat, rising and then—God help him—reaching out to take his hand.

A wiser man might have kept the conversation going between them. Might have spelled things out rather than jumping straight into bed.

Sadly, Blake didn't have enough blood in his brain to play the part of the wise man. And he wasn't convinced it was necessary.

Erika was the one who always needed to talk things out, to lay all the cards on the table, while he tended to lead with his instincts, going with the flow. He was impulse to her structure, spontaneous to her organization. Together, they were both sides of the coin, the yin and the yang, the peanut butter and the jelly.

He'd waited for this moment for three long years, and now that it was here, he wasn't about to delay a second more. If Erika didn't need to discuss it, then *he* sure as shit didn't.

He turned her once they were in the bedroom and before she could process his intention, he had her shirt off and on the floor by their feet. Within seconds, her bra was with it.

Blake's gaze traveled down as he fought to catch his breath, kicking himself for letting so much time pass without claiming this woman as his.

If anyone had asked him a month ago about his life, he would have described it as perfect. Wonderful family, dream job, great teammates, and the best friend anyone could ever ask for living across the hall.

He'd literally been the biggest dumbass on the planet.

"Blake," she whispered, looking at him through those long, thick lashes. "I want you."

He closed his eyes and thanked every deity ever worshipped.

"I want you too."

Then he lowered his head, pressed his lips to hers, and showed her just how damn much.

* * *

Erika tried to draw in a breath, tried to steady herself. She wasn't sure what had possessed her to rattle off her entire crappy romantic history to him, but once she started sharing, she couldn't stop. Because no one knew her as well as Blake did. Not even her parents. Once she began filling in the missing pieces, it just felt right, opening that door, letting him see every single part of her.

She wasn't sure where that confidence was coming from. If anything, sharing all her romance horror stories should have solidified just how shit she was at finding a man who would look at her, see the real her, and not let his gaze drift around immediately in search of someone else.

The thing was…when she'd come out of the bedroom earlier, when Blake had lifted his eyes, she'd felt seen. Truly seen.

But more than that, she'd felt *wanted*.

Sensible Erika should stop kissing Blake until they'd nailed down some answers. Like what he thought was going on here, what his intentions were. Like whether this was a one-time thing or a casual fling or…*please God*, more.

Unfortunately, Blake's kiss was drawing out the less frequently seen Wild Erika, the one she kept under lock and key twenty-four-seven. That version of herself didn't give two fucks about the whys behind this.

Maybe tomorrow she'd open her eyes and realize this was a mistake.

God, she was probably definitely going to do that. But she couldn't find it in herself to give a damn. Blake was right. All that mattered was here and now.

His hands cupped her cheeks in a way that made her feel cherished and possessed all at the same time. Blake's tongue slipped inside her mouth, the two of them sharing each other's taste. Beer and pizza. Delicious.

"I could stand here and kiss you all night," he murmured against her lips.

As good as all night sounded, Erika had gone way too long without a lover. Blake's masturbation lesson had only whetted her desire for something more, something real. Using her toys on herself might scratch an itch, but it didn't set every nerve ending in her body on fire, the way Blake was right now with a passionate kiss.

Finally, he pulled away, both of them drawing in some much-needed air. When he bent his head, clearly intent on continuing the kissing, she pulled away slightly.

His kisses were magic, but they weren't enough. Not right now, when it felt as if someone had detonated a bomb in her body, her pussy, her nipples, and every other freaking erogenous zone ricocheting with desires that bordered on painful.

All she wanted was him.

Inside her.

Now.

Blake chuckled. "Demanding much?"

Erika frowned. Fuck. Had she said that out loud? Guess there was no point in playing shy or coy now.

"Blake. Please." She was helpless to shield the neediness in her tone.

Blake tugged off his hoodie, the two of them naked from the waist up. While Erika had seen him shirtless countless times, she'd never been free to study him, to touch him, to taste. Bending forward, she placed a kiss just over his heart, then she drew her lips to the right, teasing the tight brown nub of his nipple with her tongue.

Blake's chest was completely bare, and fuck if it didn't look like it was chiseled in stone. He was a Greek god brought to life, sent down from Olympus.

He reached for the button on her jeans. Erika resisted the urge to rear back, her heart racing with arousal and the tiniest bit of nervousness. While she wanted to be here, that annoying, mean-spirited voice in the back of her head was telling her she was crazy to think she could keep up with someone like Blake in the bedroom.

Her sexual experiences were solely of the vanilla variety, leaving her with nothing more than a lifetime of missionary and doggie style under her belt.

The silence in the room was filled by the sound of Blake pulling down the zipper on her jeans. He tucked his large, calloused hands inside the denim, inside the lace of her panties, then he slowly pushed them down together. He followed, kneeling before her, lifting one foot and then the other to drag them off.

He remained there for a moment before rising again.

Her eyes met his.

Last night, when he'd dried her off and dressed her, he'd kept his gaze *mostly* locked on her face, playing the gentleman.

That guy was gone. Now that she was completely naked, Blake took a step back, his eyes traveling from head to toe then back again, stopping for longer glances of her tits and pussy.

"You're so beautiful."

She smiled at his compliment, until his look of awe flattened out, a scowl taking its place. Moving closer, he lifted her arm, turning it carefully, his fingertips stroking the skin.

"You have bruises," he said, that dark and dangerous tone she'd heard this morning returning as he took in the result of Doug's rough handling. Releasing one arm, he scowled at the bruises on the other as well.

"Kiss them better," she whispered.

Her words had the effect she'd hoped for as the two of them laughed breathlessly, recalling the night Blake made a similar request after his fight on the ice.

He did exactly as she asked, his lips so soft on the sore spots, he made her a believer, convincing her kisses really could heal.

She cupped his cheek. It was stubbled, a true five-o'clock shadow, his typical look. The only exception was the full beard he sported during playoffs, when no one on the team shaved, holding to that belief—superstition—that hockey should be their singular focus and personal hygiene is nothing more than a distraction.

"You know," she said softly, "this hero thing of yours is sort of starting to become a habit."

"I like taking care of you," he confessed, and she knew without a shadow of a doubt he meant it. Blake didn't view her as helpless. If he had, she never would have let him do as much for her as she did.

"Kiss me," she whispered, loving the way the mere touch of his lips against hers took away every bad thought and feeling she'd been having lately.

Blake didn't grant her request. Instead, he pulled down the duvet and gestured toward the bed. "Crawl in first."

She did as he said, her haste causing him to chuckle.

"You're so perfect, Erik."

She sat in the middle of her bed, watching as Blake toed off his shoes, then unfastened his jeans.

Erika forgot to breathe as he lowered the denim and his boxers together. "Oh!"

"Told you that dildo was small," he joked.

She hadn't believed that until now, but hell would freeze over before she admitted that to her cocky bestie.

Blake grinned, then he climbed into the bed. Tugging on her ankle, he used his strength—good God, the man was built like an ox—to pull her down until she was flat on her back. Then he crawled over her, caging her beneath him, giving her that kiss she'd requested.

Unable to resist, Erika decided to treat herself to a little bit of exploring, her hands touching his bare chest and midriff before roaming around to stroke his back and the top of his firm ass.

There wasn't a soft part on the guy. Literally, no part of him didn't feel like pure steel.

Blake's hands cupped the sides of her head so he could use his grip to deepen their kiss. She'd never been kissed so hard or so long. The edges of her vision turned gray from the lack of air, and she started to feel light-headed.

She would have twisted away, sucking in some deep breaths, but Blake didn't appear to be in a hurry to move them on to the next part.

Releasing her, he placed a few more soft kisses on her cheeks, the tip of her nose, even her chin. "What are you thinking about?"

She frowned. Thinking? "Uh…"

Blake gave her a cat-who-ate-the-canary grin. "So, nothing. That's my girl. Just wanted to make sure you weren't making some sort of list in your head."

Erika believed in giving credit where credit was due. "No lists. Just thinking about you. And those kisses. Did you take a class or something? Major in kissing, because I've never… No one has ever…"

She expected Blake to laugh at her joke, but his gaze sharpened, his expression turning serious. "I've never kissed anyone like this, Erik. Fuck, I don't even usually *like* kissing, but with you…I can't stop myself. It's like you and your lips are a drug, and I'm already hooked."

Erika blinked a couple times, trying to process his confession. "I'm your drug?"

How awesome was that?

"Mmm-hmm," he hummed, giving her another kiss. This one was softer than the last five hundred, but no less powerful, no less potent.

As blown away as Erika was by his kisses, they were wreaking havoc on her libido, driving her arousal to dangerous heights.

"Please," she murmured against his mouth.

"Please what?"

"Blake. I want you."

His lips left hers, traveling across her cheek to her ear. "I know it's been a long time since…"

Erika sighed, reading the concern on his face. Even in bed, Blake couldn't seem to turn off that caregiver gene. Unfortunately, it was misplaced and unwanted here. So she offered a tip she suspected would get her the results she desired. "I haven't had sex in three and a half years, Blake. So much time has passed, I've learned to live without it."

"Live without it?" he repeated, scowling as if she'd said something wrong.

"Yep."

Blake chuckled darkly. "Oh, Erik. I'm going to prove to you exactly how ridiculous that statement is."

If she weren't so freaking horny, she'd call him to task for being a smug ass. However, she was also kind of afraid he would do exactly what he said. After all, his masturbation lesson had lit a bonfire inside her, and he'd barely even touched her, letting the toys do the heavy lifting.

Reaching toward her nightstand, he withdrew her nearly expired condoms. "Hate to see these go to waste."

She laughed. "Made it just under the wire."

Blake pulled one from the box, tearing the package open with his teeth and donning the condom. She expected him to get right down to business.

But like everything about Blake, he took her by surprise, sliding down the length of her body, pressing her legs open and kneeling between them, his face even with her pussy.

"What are you—" That was all she managed to say before he sucked her clit into his mouth. "Ah!" Her hands flew to his hair as she sought something to hold on to. Blake's lips, tongue, and teeth should be declared lethal weapons.

"You're going to come on my mouth for the first orgasm, Erik."

She closed her eyes, seriously praying because she wasn't sure how many of Blake's orgasms she could survive. He'd given her two that night with her toys, and she'd fallen into the deepest sleep of her life. Something told her he was going to go for broke this time around.

Her fingers clenched in his hair, and he hissed.

"Sorry," she murmured, loosening them.

Blake shook his head. "Keep holding on tight," he demanded. "I don't mind a little pain."

She didn't intend to follow that directive, but Blake took the decision away from her when he nipped at her clit, biting down until she wriggled, trying to decide if it hurt or felt amazing. That internal debate ended when he pushed two thick fingers inside her, fucking her into oblivion as she grasped his hair, holding on for dear life.

Her back arched as she came, her body shaking like a giant freight train. Blake drew the climax out, his fingers not stilling until he'd wrung out every drop of exquisite pleasure.

Erika's hands fell away from his hair, her eyes closed as she tried to catch her breath. She felt rather than saw Blake climbing over her once more.

His lips found hers, and she tasted herself on them and on his tongue.

Again, she expected him to move to the next part, but Blake still didn't appear to be in any hurry. He kissed her like a man with nothing but time on his hands.

When she opened her eyes, he broke the kiss and smiled at her. "You back?"

She nodded, suddenly realizing he'd been giving her time to recover.

"Good. Because I didn't want you to miss a second of this." Blake guided the head of his dick to her opening. "You're so hot, Erik. And wet. God, I could drown in here."

She loved the way he talked dirty to her. She wished she had the ability to do the same, but her vocabulary while in bed with him seemed limited to two words. His name and "please."

"Blake."

It was all she had to say. He pressed inside, one long, relentless thrust that didn't stop until he was fully seated.

"God!" she cried out, tilting her hips, aware that he hadn't even started fucking her yet and she was already wondering how in the hell she'd gone so long without this.

Blake dropped to his elbows, pressing his chest against her breasts. He resumed those heady kisses from before while his hips lifted and fell, his cock pistoning inside her in a way she'd never experienced.

Sex before Blake had been too tame, too boring, the equivalent of sitting in the doctor's waiting room thirty minutes past the time of her appointment.

Sex *with* Blake was a parade, a rock concert, and a hit Broadway show, all rolled into one.

He fucked her through one orgasm, slowing his thrusts but not stopping as she lay beneath him, certain one more of those mind-blowing climaxes would kill her.

Once she recovered, he withdrew, flipping her to her stomach like she was his own personal rag doll. Lifting her hips, he returned—fucking her like a man possessed.

And throughout it all, he murmured a litany of all the dirty, kinky, amazing things he was going to do to her, vowing they hadn't even begun to scratch the surface.

Jesus! She'd never been taken with this kind of force. It was the single hottest experience of her life. Her third orgasm came at her from out of nowhere, figuratively knocking her on her ass, her inner muscles clenching so hard, she saw stars.

Blake cursed. "That's right, Erik. Fucking hell, you sexy dirty girl. You're squeezing me so tight, feels like you're going to crush my dick."

She trembled as the climax waned, every ounce of strength drained from her body. Not that Blake seemed to notice or care.

He withdrew again, flipping her to her back again. "One more time. Let me see those pretty eyes of yours when you come with me."

She shook her head. Or she should say, her head flopped just twice as she gave him a great impersonation of a fish on the shore.

"One more," he repeated in that dark tone that warned he was going to get his way.

"I'll die."

He pushed his cock back inside. "I'll bring you back to life if you do," he promised. His thrusts were slower this time, but even more forceful.

"I really don't…think…I can…" she said, fighting to draw air into her lungs.

Blake didn't acknowledge her protest. Instead, he tilted her hips, dragging her legs over his shoulders. This position was a killer, because on the next stroke—

"What the hell?" she gasped.

"G-spot," he replied, hitting it again and again.

She'd never met that fellow before, but damn if she didn't like him. *A lot*.

"Oh my God!" Apparently, her body hadn't gotten the memo that she was finished with orgasms, because in less than a dozen more thrusts, every single one hitting *that* spot, she fell off the cliff for the fourth time, and mercifully, Blake followed her down.

They remained there, connected, neither speaking for several minutes, just staring into each other's eyes, before Blake finally withdrew and dropped down next to her on the mattress.

"Still think you can live without sex?"

Erika grinned. "I don't think I can survive the next twenty *minutes* without it."

Blake laughed loudly. "Set a timer for fifteen minutes, Erik. Because I'm definitely going to do whatever it takes to keep my girl alive."

CHAPTER ELEVEN

BLAKE LAY with his eyes closed, though he wasn't asleep. Erika was resting quietly in his arms, using his chest as a pillow. After round two of the greatest sex of his life, they'd curled up together, and while neither of them was sleeping, it felt as if they were both taking some time to just wallow in this…bliss.

"Mmm." Erika lifted her head. "What time is it?"

Blake picked up her phone from the nightstand. "Midnight."

"Can't believe I'm not sound asleep," she murmured.

"Someone wear you out?"

She laughed softly. "And then some."

He chuckled. "I swear to God I'm less worn out after three periods on the ice. That was quite a workout, Dr. Nelson."

"No one's ever…" she started, her words fading away.

"No one's ever," he prompted.

She flushed slightly, grinning. "No one's ever managed to give me more than one orgasm in a night. No one's ever found my G-spot, and *none* of my past boyfriends managed to use my clit to its full potential."

Blake cupped her cheek, giving her a quick kiss. "Not gonna complain about coming out on top in any competition, even though the thought of you with those other guys makes me see red."

"Never pegged you for the jealous type," she teased.

Because he wasn't. Or he hadn't been. Before her. Now he was feeling uncharacteristically caveman-like.

He drew his fingers over her bare shoulder, then tugged her closer. "What do you say we get a shower, then call it a night?"

Erika pushed to a sitting position. "A shower together?"

Blake grinned at her obvious excitement. "I dare you to try to take one without me."

She gave him a quick kiss on the lips, then climbed out of bed, padding to the bathroom. She stopped at the doorway. "Dare you."

Blake leapt from the bed, much to Erika's delight, chasing her into the bathroom. Within sixty seconds, they were standing together underneath the steaming jets.

Erika threw her head back to wet her long dark hair. She started to reach for the shampoo, but Blake beat her to it. Squeezing some onto the palm of his hand, he gestured for her to turn around.

"You're going to wash my hair?" she asked, clearly pleased by the prospect.

"I'm going to wash every inch of you." He placed a kiss on the top of her head. "And then you're going to repay the favor."

Erika glanced over her shoulder, her eyes heavy with need. He'd never really understood the term *bedroom eyes* until that moment, when she flashed him a seductive look that woke his dick up fast. A fact that didn't go unnoticed as her eyes drifted down his body, a smile crossing her lips.

"Keep looking at me like that and this shower is going to be less about getting clean and more about getting very, very dirty," he murmured.

"Cleanliness is overrated."

This woman was made for him. Blake ran his fingers through her hair, working up a lather before turning her to face him so he could tip her head back to rinse the suds out. Her breasts were pressed against his chest, his cock bumping against her stomach. Once the shampoo was out, he repeated the process with her conditioner.

Erika's hands gripped his waist, and she kept leaning forward to lick stray drops of water that slid down his chest. It was one of the most erotically charged moments he'd ever experienced. Once her hair was washed, he grabbed her loofah, squirting a generous amount of body wash on the surface.

He was familiar with her sweet scent, something he often caught whiffs of whenever she stopped by his place after showering. He'd never really considered a smell a turn-on, but there was no denying—he glanced at the bottle—white peach and rice milk was going to give him hard-ons from this point on.

Blake ran the loofah over her shoulders, neck, and back.

"Oh my God, that feels so good," Erika said.

"It really does," he agreed, enjoying her slight intake of breath when he drew the loofah down her spine and over her ass. "Turn around so I can rinse off the soap."

She twisted to face him again, the hot water sluicing down her back. Now he could focus his attention on the front. He dropped the loofah, opting for a more hands-on cleaning approach, running his fingers through her slit.

"So wet for me," he said, bending forward to kiss the side of her neck.

Erika didn't reply with words but with whimpers when he found and circled her clit, applying enough pressure to fire her engines without blasting off. Their first two times together had been explosive, but Blake hadn't taken nearly enough time to savor the experience.

Now that they'd sated their immediate hunger, he was ready for a leisurely dessert.

He shifted lower, bending at the waist. The new position meant he could suck her nipple into his mouth as he stroked along her slit and toyed with her clit.

Erika's hands rested on his shoulders, her fingers digging into the muscles there as she pushed her body forward, seeking more.

"Please, Blake," she whispered.

He knew what she wanted, knew she was asking him to fill her with his fingers or his dick.

"You're going to have to beg a lot more than that before you get what you want, dirty girl," he taunted.

Her eyes had been closed, but now they flew open, piercing him with a demanding look that made him laugh. His little kitten thought she had claws.

Blake placed a kiss on the tip of her nose. "You're so adorable when you think you can make me do something."

"You realize I had an excellent tutor in the ways of masturbation." She lowered her hands from his shoulders, sliding her fingers over her breasts and stomach seductively. "I don't need you to—"

That was all she managed to say before he grasped her wrists, shoving her back against the shower wall, cutting off her words with a hard, claiming kiss. He surprised her with his rough touch, her moans music to his ears. Erika liked her pleasure with a bite of pain, and he suddenly imagined her draped over his lap while he spanked her ass. Or tied to the bed as he tormented her with her toys for hours on end. Or maybe he'd buy her a butt plug, introduce her to anal.

While they hadn't discussed it outright, he gathered her past lovers hadn't branched out in terms of testing Erika's sexual limits. Blake wouldn't make the same mistake.

Now that he had her, a whole world of sexual adventures was open to them.

Breaking off the kiss, he nipped at her lower lip, her arms still lifted and pressed against the tiles over her head.

"*My* pussy," he growled. "You don't touch it without my permission."

Erika's eyes narrowed. She was feminist enough to want to

protest that statement, but her flushed cheeks and labored breathing gave her away.

"Tell me," Blake insisted. "Tell me whose pussy this is."

She bit her lip, but he knew the act had nothing to do with nervousness. His headstrong woman was trying to stop herself from giving in too quick.

"Say it, Erik, and I'll give you your first orgasm now."

"First?" she whispered.

"There's lots of hot water left."

"Yours." It was one word, spoken more with air than tone, but Blake heard it, and it sent him to his knees instantly, ready to prove to her just how true that was.

Erika's hands gripped his hair as he used his thumbs to part her folds. He sucked her clit into his mouth hard, then gave it a nip, and she cried out.

He repeated the same thing several times, driving her higher and higher, yet she begged for more.

"Blake! God. I need… I need…"

He knew exactly what she needed. He shoved two fingers deep inside her, not bothering to with light or easy. When he curved his fingers, finding that spot that Erika hadn't even discovered herself, the bomb detonated and her orgasm had her bending forward, beautifully broken by pleasure.

"*Jesus.*" Her climax struck hard, but he wasn't content to let it flash out too quickly, so he kept fucking her, drawing it out, wanting it to linger as long as possible.

Once it waned, Blake stood, his hands gripping her upper arms to hold her upright. She was also using the wall at her back for support.

"That was…"

He didn't have a clue what she was going to say. Maybe she didn't either. Or maybe she realized words weren't going to cut it because one second, she was standing there, looking at him like he was the most special person in her life, and the next, she was on her knees.

Blake jerked in surprise when she grasped his cock, her lips wrapping around the head at the same time.

"Fuck!" His hands flew to her head. He thought his intention was to slow her down, but somewhere between lifting his hands and fisting her hair, she'd wiped that decision away.

Erika drew him in until the head of his cock brushed the back of her throat, then she pulled away, only for a second, before sucking him down again. She ran her tongue along the underside of his dick on each withdrawal, adding a sensation that was going to make him come way too fucking fast.

When her hand found its way between his legs, cupping his balls, he had to lock his knees and grit his teeth, fighting for control.

Her whimper reverberated around his cock, drawing his attention to her, and that was when he realized he was pulling her hair, using it to guide her depth, to set the pace. He'd inadvertently taken this from blowjob to mouth fucking.

Blake loosened his grip, and Erika's eyes rose, meeting his as she shook her head as much as possible with her mouth full of him.

"I was hurting you," he murmured.

She rolled her eyes, the expression on her face one he'd seen countless times in the past. It was her "get a grip, Blake" expression, and it took everything he had not to laugh.

He probably would have if she hadn't chosen that exact moment to toss gasoline onto the fire—the tip of her finger circling his anus.

Game. Fucking. On.

Blake closed his fists in her hair, resuming his earlier pace, then bumping it up a notch when Erika tried to wrestle back control.

"Your mouth is mine too," he said through gritted teeth.

Erika hummed her assent, wiggled her finger against his ass, then tightened her grip on the base of his cock.

It was too much and not enough all at the same time because

he didn't want to come alone. He wanted her with him. Every damn time.

"Stroke your clit," he demanded, partly for her pleasure, but also as a distraction because he was in serious danger of blowing right now.

Her finger disappeared from where it had been toying with his anus, and he missed it immediately. Then her breathing grew heavier, and he could tell she was doing what he'd asked, even though he couldn't see.

"You're going to come with me."

Erika looked up again, uncertain.

"I'm not giving you an option. Stroke your clit, get yourself close."

Her eyes drifted closed, though he wasn't sure if it was her fingers or the way he was using her mouth or maybe both, working against her.

Though he'd only seen her come undone a handful of times, he was starting to recognize her tells…the harsh breaths, the flushed cheeks, the breathy groans when she was close.

"Three fingers," he said, his voice husky with need. "Fuck yourself with three, dirty girl."

Erika moaned and trembled.

"Fuck yourself the way I would. Hard and fast and rough. Get that pussy nice and wet and messy." He prayed to God she got there quick because he was on the cusp and there wasn't enough control in the world to stop him from—

Erika's cries were muffled by his cock, her body shaking as her orgasm struck. He was only two thrusts behind her, then he came. She didn't release him, didn't shy away. Instead, she held him in her mouth until every drop was spent, and only then did she pull away and—fuck him—swallow.

He reached down, helping her to her feet, wrapping her in his arms. She sank into his embrace, and it was then that Blake realized their hot shower was no more than lukewarm, the water quickly turning cold.

He switched the faucet off, leaning her against the wall as he stepped out and grabbed a towel. Blake dried her off, the moment reminding him of the night she'd lost Corky in the storm. She'd looked so defeated, so broken that night.

None of that was present now.

Right now, she looked well fucked, happy, and sleepy.

She didn't move until he'd dried every part of her and himself. When he held out his hand, she took it, a soft smile on her lips.

"That was…"

He chuckled. "Yeah. It was."

They walked back into her bedroom, crawling into bed together, both grinning when Corky hopped up, claiming her own spot at the bottom.

Erika started to nestle into his arms, but he turned her away from him instead so he could wrap his arm around her waist, spooning her. He had a feeling this was going to be their favorite sleeping position.

He lifted his hand, cupping her breast, provoking a breathy laugh from her, but she didn't seek to lower it or push it away. Quite the opposite as his shameless, sexy minx wiggled her ass, pressing it more firmly against him.

Blake was amused when he realized she'd fallen asleep within seconds, but it didn't last long. He only had time to think about how perfectly they fit together before he joined her in dreamland.

* * *

Buzz. Buzz. Buzz.

Blake waved his hand toward the nightstand, trying to stop the buzzing. It was too fucking early for phone calls, especially considering the late night he and Erika had.

"Make it stop," she muttered from beside him, her face buried in a pillow.

On the third wild swing, Blake's hand connected with the nightstand. He dragged his fingers across the surface until he found the vibrating phone. Lifting it, he took one glance at the screen, then nudged Erika on the shoulder.

"It's the hospital calling your cell," he said.

She groaned, then took it from him just as the buzzing stopped.

"It's five in the fucking morning," he pointed out.

"I know. If they call back—" she started, just as the phone began to vibrate again, and this time she answered.

The hospital didn't call her on her off-hours often, but when they were short-staffed and desperate, they had a tendency to ring her phone off the hook until she answered.

"Okay," he heard her say to whoever had called. "I'll be there as soon as I can."

She disconnected the call, slowly sitting up and rubbing her face with her hands.

"You gotta go?" He blamed his stupid question on the fact it was too freaking early. Obviously, she was leaving.

Erika rose, walking to the bathroom to turn on the light. "Apparently it's foggy out there. Big accident on 695, ten-car pileup. Lots of injuries. They're transporting them now."

"You only got four hours' sleep," he grumbled.

Blake covered his eyes for a moment, blinking a few times to adjust to the light shining in his face before forcing himself to move. Corky was still asleep at their feet, and even she seemed to understand it was basically still night because aside from opening her eyes, she didn't stir or even bother to lift her head.

Erika peered through the door, looking surprisingly alert. "I'll take a nap when I get home."

Blake scrubbed his face, trying to wake himself. Then he threw his legs over the side of the mattress. Erika had grabbed some clothes from her dresser before heading to the bathroom, leaving the door open.

"You don't have to get up," she said. "Sleep a little longer."

He shook his head. "No. I'll make you some coffee in a travel mug. Then I need to get back to my place to pack anyway. Got a ten a.m. flight to Vegas."

"Oh," she said. "That's right. You're on the road for a few days."

Blake had hoped they'd have time for a quickie, breakfast, and then a talk before he had to head out.

He really should have initiated the conversation last night. The one they still hadn't had yet.

Not that he thought it was necessary. Erika had been all-in for their sexcapades, and there'd been no question after their shower that he was spending the night. They hadn't needed to discuss anything because the last piece of the puzzle had finally snapped into place.

He'd been secretly pleased and relieved that Erika hadn't needed to spell everything out between them. Perhaps she—like him—had finally realized they were perfect for each other.

If she hadn't, there was no way she would have let things between them advance to the next level without a lot—and he meant A LOT—of talking.

Everything they'd done since dinner had held way more weight than a bunch of words. Why say the words when they could simply show each other how they felt?

Padding to the kitchen barefoot, Blake grabbed a travel mug from her cabinet and pressed the button on the Nespresso to brew the coffee, adding creamer and sugar the way she liked. He'd just popped the top on when she came out of the bedroom, fully dressed and ready to go. He could see from the pensive look on her face she was already thinking about what she would be facing at the hospital. He'd become a bit of an expert over the years in reading Erika's expressions, so he knew her worried doctor face.

"Here," he said, holding the coffee cup out to her once she'd thrown on her coat and grabbed her purse and car keys.

"I'm sorry I have to run like this."

Blake leaned forward and gave her a kiss on the cheek. "It's okay. I would have had to leave in a couple hours anyway. I'll see you when I get back."

It looked as if Erika wanted to say something more, but in the end, she just nodded. "Safe flight," she said, just as she had a million times before.

Unfortunately, this time…something felt slightly off.

Before Blake could reach for her, intent on giving her a proper kiss goodbye, Erika turned toward the door. "See you in a few days."

He frowned, annoyed. What the hell kind of goodbye was that?

He shook it off, chalking it up to her rush to get to the hospital. Obviously, there were a lot of people who needed her help. When he considered that, he felt selfish for trying to steal a few more minutes.

Sighing, he returned to her bedroom, pulling his phone from the jeans he'd shed last night. He fired off a quick text. Given Erika's lacking relationship history, it appeared it was up to him to show her how a decent boyfriend treated his girlfriend.

The irony of that wasn't lost on him because God knew he had less experience than *she* did with committed relationships.

Regardless…he was willing to give it the old college try.

> Miss you already. Hope everything is okay at the hospital. I'll text when I land. Dream of me tonight, because I'm sure as hell going to be dreaming of you.

Blake hit send, grinning. Not too bad if he said so himself. He waited for the three dots to appear, just in case Erika hadn't gotten to her car yet.

When they didn't, he figured she was already driving. She'd dealt with too many injuries thanks to distracted driving, so she never looked at her phone when she was behind the wheel.

* * *

"Who pissed in your Cheerios this morning?" Tank stowed his bag in the overhead compartment of the plane before plopping down next to Blake. They were heading back to Baltimore after three days bouncing around the West Coast, starting in Vegas before moving on to San Jose. Finally, they were on their way home.

All Blake had to do was get this six-and-a-half-hour flight over with, then he could get back home to his girls.

Or at least, he *hoped* they were his girls. He didn't question Corky's devotion to him, but it felt like he might be on shaky ground with Erika.

No. Not shaky.

Just the same fucking ground he'd been on for the past three years. When he left her place after what he was now calling the greatest night of his life, his feet didn't touch the ground for hours. In his mind, he and Erika had turned a corner, had embarked on what he hoped was going to be his first—and, God willing, last—serious committed relationship.

"I'm fine," he lied to Tank, though his crossed arms and scowl were probably belying that fact.

"Dude," Tank said with an arched brow. "You just played two of the best fucking games of your career, and you've set yourself up to break your own personal scoring record. Not to mention if you score forty goals, it'll be your third consecutive year doing so, which means you'll be tied with Alex Stone, who currently holds the record for the Rays. You're on fire this season."

Blake tried not to think about stuff like that too hard because fixating on records could fuck with a guy's head. "I don't look at the numbers, you know that."

"I get it," Tank hastened to add. Probably because his best friend was also in line to tie Stone's record, and like Blake, he knew it was best to take it one game at a time rather than start obsessing about the bigger picture. "Just trying to figure out why you're doing a damn good impersonation of Victor this morning. Because you've got his scowl down, man."

"I fucking heard that," Victor grumbled from across the aisle.

Coulton, who had the window seat, peered around Victor and chuckled. "Tank's right. Blake looks just like you right now. Grumpy as fuck."

"I'm not grumpy," Victor grumbled. "I just don't like people."

"You're surrounded by your team," Tank pointed out. "It's not like you're flying coach alone."

Victor rolled his eyes. "You're still fucking people."

They'd all been friends for way too long to take offense to anything Victor said.

Tank turned back to Blake. "I can only assume you've stalled out with Erika. So I guess it's my job as best friend to offer you your choices. Do something about it, or you'll be back to taking victory laps with Mindy."

"Mindy." Blake shook his head in disgust. "No fucking way."

Tank crossed his arms. "It's not like you've made any progress on the Erika front, and Mindy's been complaining about you not calling her anymore."

"You know I'm not sleeping with Mindy. Ever again," Blake insisted, feeling slightly guilty for not clueing his best friend into the fact he *had* taken a step forward with Erika. Of course, it had been followed by two steps back, but Tank didn't know that either.

"Damn," Tank muttered, his tone catching Blake off guard.

"Damn?"

He sighed. "I made the mistake of taking her home one night, and she's been fucking clingy ever since. Did you know she can tie herself up in bed?"

Blake was all too aware of that party trick.

Coulton's eyes widened. "Seriously?"

Tank and Blake both nodded.

"That's fucking weird," Victor said, his words matching Blake's opinion. "If I want a woman tied to my bed, you can be damn sure I'm going to be the one tightening the fucking knots."

Tank laughed loudly, reaching across the aisle to punch Victor on the arm. "I knew you were a kinky bastard."

Victor growled but didn't deny the accusation.

"Seriously, Blake. What's going on?" Coulton asked. "You're the one who's usually in a big-ass hurry to get home to that damn dog."

Blake hadn't told any of his friends about his night with Erika. He wasn't sure why, but now…when he considered it…he thought maybe it was because he didn't want to jinx it until it was all sorted out and official. He'd had a niggling feeling that wasn't the case when she'd left to go the hospital, so he'd kept his mouth shut.

Now that niggling feeling had taken over, growing to a 9.0 earthquake on the Richter scale.

"Is it that guy Erika's seeing?" Tank asked. "Is it more serious?"

Blake also hadn't told them about Doug attacking Erika because he hadn't known how to share that story without sliding into the aftermath. Now, though, he was ready to come clean about everything…because he needed his friends' advice.

"It's a long story." He started by telling them about losing Corky, leaving out the part about Erika's intense fear of storms because that was too personal. Instead, he said they'd both been freaked out over losing the puppy and had fallen asleep at his place.

"You two and that fucking dog," Victor muttered.

Then he told them about the next morning, about Doug hitting Erika, shaking her. Blake had never questioned how solid his friendship with his teammates was, but if he had any doubts, they were erased by the sheer murder in their eyes when they learned Erika had been hurt.

"What's Doug's fucking last name?" Victor asked through gritted teeth.

"Where does he live?" Coulton looked equally deadly.

Blake wished he knew the answers to those questions. "I punched him, probably broke his nose."

Tank scowled. "That's not enough."

"Fucking tell me about it," Blake agreed. "Anyway, I comforted her, but then I had to leave for practice, so we made plans for dinner later."

"You two eat dinner together most nights. So what?" Tank asked.

"We had sex."

His words evoked three very different responses from his buddies. Coulton looked shocked, Victor scowled, and Tank—true to character—slapped him on the arm, grinning from ear to ear.

"Hot fucking damn! Hell yeah!" Tank shouted, drawing the attention of two flight attendants, both shooting him a warning look to hold it down. It didn't help that he'd expressed his glee during the safety demonstration.

"Why are we just hearing about all of this?" Coulton asked. "We've been together for days."

Blake lifted one shoulder. "I don't know."

"Fuck." Victor leaned across the aisle to ask quietly, "Was the sex bad?"

Blake quickly shook his head, putting that thought to rest immediately. "Hell no. It was..." Even though he was worried about the current situation between him and his gorgeous neighbor, he couldn't hold back the smile that emerged every single time he recalled being with her.

Tank laughed. "Clearly, the sex was shit-hot."

"That's a fucking relief," Victor said.

"It's just...I don't know. I thought things had changed between us, but the last few days, the texts—"

"Sexts?" Tank interjected, wiggling his brows.

Blake shook his head. "Texts. Just matter-of-fact, run-of-the-mill texts. The same kind of texts we've been exchanging for years. And there haven't been very many. Shit, she even ghosted me one whole day. It's starting to feel like Erika has shoved me back into the friend box."

"What did she say when you told her you wanted to date her exclusively, wanted her to be your girlfriend?" Coulton asked.

Blake grimaced.

"Fucking hell," Victor muttered. "You did fucking tell her?"

"I was going to." Blake tried to defend himself, even though he knew he didn't have a leg to stand on. "I planned on sitting down with her at breakfast the morning after and laying it all out. My feelings, my hopes for our future, but..."

"But?" Coulton prodded.

"She got called into the hospital for an emergency at five in the morning. One minute, she was asleep in my arms. Five minutes later, she was in her car, driving to work."

"But you've been texting her the past three days," Tank pointed out.

Blake glanced down at his phone. "Yeah. The first day I sent her a bunch of texts, talking about how much I missed her and couldn't wait to see her again."

"Sounds nice," Coulton observed.

"She didn't text me back until the middle of the night, which was weird. I was sacked out in the hotel and didn't see it until the next morning. And then that day, she ghosted me."

"What did her text say?" Tank asked.

"She just asked if we won against Vegas, then said she and Corky missed me too."

"She didn't watch the game?" Tank asked.

The same time Victor asked, "Corky? Who gives a fuck about the dog's feelings?"

"I do," Blake retorted. "But it was just such a generic text. And the fact that she didn't watch the game...I don't know. It got in my head, you know? So I texted back, but…well…I was reluctant to…"

"You fell back on the old Blake material instead of putting yourself out there." Coulton looked like he understood, even though there was the slightest bit of disappointment in his gaze.

"She didn't start texting me back until yesterday morning, but it was the standard stuff, couple of pics of Corky, she wished me luck in the game, shit like that. She's always said since day one she just wanted us to be friends, and I got that. Or…" Blake hastened to add, when all three of his friends shot him a "seriously?" look. "I *thought* I was getting it. I haven't exactly helped my case with her, bringing home puck bunnies for victory dances, swearing off marriage, strutting around like an arrogant playboy."

"Yeah, but you had sex. I mean…she slept with you. What the hell does she think that means?" Coulton asked.

Blake left Baltimore feeling good about where he and Erika were, but each day since, he'd been looking at things from *her* perspective…and not liking what he was coming up with. "Well, worst-case scenario—she thinks it was a one-night stand. Although, maybe that's not the worst case because what I'm really afraid of is she views what we did as me trying to console and comfort her."

"With sex?" Tank chuckled. "Nice."

"No, you fucking idiot." Victor reached over and cuffed Tank on the back of the head. "Because that's what Blake always does. He takes care of Erika. Making sure she eats dinner, fixing shit in her apartment, fucking adopting a dog with her because she always wanted a dog."

Blake was shocked that Victor had noticed all that, even though his words were all true. He *had* placed himself in the role of caregiver, which was strange because he'd sure as shit never wanted to take care of anyone else in his life. With Erika, that desire came naturally because he only ever wanted her to be happy, well-fed, safe, and loved.

Victor shook his head at Tank, but it was Blake he was looking at when he said, "Actually, *you're* the fucking idiot. Spent a whole night with that woman and couldn't find ten seconds to tell her you loved her."

Blake didn't respond—because there was nothing he could say in defense to that.

He *was* a fucking idiot.

CHAPTER TWELVE

ERIKA GLANCED AROUND THE ARENA. She'd gotten here earlier than she probably should have, but she'd been anxious to get out of her apartment and go somewhere that wasn't work. She was also grateful to finally feel human again.

Immediately after leaving Blake in her apartment four days earlier, she'd worked a twelve-hour shift in the ER. When they'd called her about the ten-car pileup, they had failed to mention one of the vehicles wasn't a car but a tour bus. She'd spent nearly the entire day knee-deep in injuries ranging from cuts and bruises, to whiplash, facial trauma, and broken bones, as well as too many serious head and back injuries. Four people were still in critical condition in ICU.

Unfortunately, it hadn't been the hectic, stressful workday that had done her in because she was no stranger to pulling long hours.

Nope.

What finished her was the sandwich she'd grabbed from one of the hospital vending machines. She'd gobbled it down on the way home, starving after missing breakfast and lunch. Once home, she'd hopped into the shower with plans to hit the couch in her comfies and watch Blake's game.

What she *hadn't* intended to do was to hug the toilet the entire night, praying for death.

Food poisoning was no joke.

Thank God for Ashley, who'd spent the whole next day not only taking care of Corky because Erika was practically comatose on her bathroom floor, but babysitting *her* as well, bringing her saltines and ginger ale.

After thirty-six hours of feeling like death warmed over, Erika had finally come out on the other side, only to have to return to work yesterday.

She'd been afraid Blake was upset with her for not responding to his texts. She hadn't mentioned having food poisoning to him while he was away because she didn't want to mess with his head before a game or make him worry.

She scoffed to herself because she knew the real reason—she didn't want to give him more ammunition to use against her in his campaign to teach her how to feed herself properly.

So, she was delighted when he texted earlier today to let her know he'd left a ticket for tonight's game for her at the box office.

Two of his former teammates, Alex Stone and Elio Moretti, were in town with their wives. Erika had spent more than a few nights out with both couples whenever they were in town, and Blake, the thoughtful man, knew she would enjoy watching the game with them.

As for Blake himself, they'd been playing apartment tag ever since his return from the West Coast early yesterday afternoon. She'd been at work when he returned, and by the time she'd gotten off, he'd already headed out for his stepbrother Todd's bachelor party. Todd had specifically waited to set a date for his stag night until the Rays' hockey schedule had been solidified, determined to have his big brother there for the festivities.

Erika didn't have a clue how late Blake had returned, but she'd opted not to stop in this morning, figuring he would need to sleep off the effects of the party. So she'd headed straight to work instead. Then they'd missed each other again, as Blake had been scheduled for a couple of pregame interviews, leaving for the arena before she'd returned home.

She was looking forward to finally seeing him tonight. She honestly couldn't recall the two of them ever spending so long apart, and the fact this separation came right on the heels of their night together had given her way too much time to think about —and fret over—what they'd done and what it might mean.

Blake's initial texts had been sweet and very boyfriend-like, but they'd cooled with each subsequent day until now…when it felt like they were back to being just friends again.

She was reminded of her ill-considered one-night stand with Danny, and how she'd mistakenly thought the sex had meant more than it had. It had bothered Erika when Danny finally told her point-blank he didn't want to date her, after ignoring her texts and calls.

If Blake told her he wasn't interested in more, it wouldn't bother her.

It would break her.

She blew out a frustrated breath. She'd jumped into bed with him without talking to him about what it meant. For some reason, at the time, she thought she could handle a one-night stand or casual affair with her best friend.

Where the fuck had her brain been that day?

Actually, she knew. It had been on the fritz because the whole thing with Doug had freaked her the fuck out. So much so that she'd let her needs overshadow her common sense.

Blake represented comfort and safety and…well, she liked the person she was when she was with him. Most of the world looked at her and saw a strait-laced, no-nonsense doctor, someone who was *a bit* too serious and *a lot* not fun.

Those things went away when she was with Blake. With him, she was Erik. She hung out with hockey players, ate pizza, drank beer, kicked ass at Mario Kart, and had finally—FINALLY— gotten the puppy she'd always dreamed of.

So she'd reached out for him that night. Not only because she needed him but because she wanted him. Desperately. And all his speeches about not depriving herself had finally taken root.

She didn't regret that night at all, but she sure as fuck regretted the morning after.

Ugh. This was all Blake's fault. If he'd been just as boring in bed as the rest of her ex-lovers, she might have had a fighting chance, but he'd rocked her world. Not just physically but emotionally. Everything he'd done, every word he'd said, had sunk down deep, touching all the cold, lonely places and showing her what she'd been missing her whole life.

"Hey, Erika."

Erika glanced toward the familiar female voice, smiling as Elio and Gianna Moretti entered the box. Usually when Erika attended Blake's games, she sat in one of the general admission sections, so she'd been excited about sitting in the box, complete with its own bar, wait service, and comfortable seats.

She'd been nursing a glass of red wine, though she was thinking about dumping it and ordering a ginger ale, the alcohol making her feel a touch queasy as her stomach was still on the mend from the food poisoning. She put the glass down, reaching out to accept a hug from Gianna. Once they separated, Elio leaned in and gave her a friendly kiss on the cheek.

"Good to see you again, Doc. You keeping our boy Blake in line?" he asked.

"Not sure anyone can keep him in line," she replied, uncertain if Blake had told anyone about their night together and, if so, how he'd portrayed it. Until she knew for sure, she planned to spend tonight acting as if she and Blake were just friends and no lines had been crossed.

Elio chuckled. "I keep telling him and Tank it's time to give up the puck bunnies and settle down." He wrapped his arm around his wife's shoulders. "I wasted way too many years as a bachelor."

Erika smiled, hating how jealous she felt of the lovely couple in front of her. She'd certainly never felt that way before, but suddenly she kept imagining Blake wrapping his arm around *her*, saying the same sweet words. God, how she wanted that.

"How's your daughter?" Erika asked, aware it was the perfect way to turn the conversation away from Blake.

Just as she expected, Elio's phone was instantly retrieved from his pocket, and he was scrolling through pictures of their little girl. Erika had to admit, Elio and Gianna had made one adorable baby.

"She's so stinking cute," Erika gushed sincerely.

"Jesus. How long did it take him to pull the phone out?" Alex asked, as he and his wife, Charley, entered the box and joined them.

Erika and Gianna exchanged a glance, grinning.

"Three minutes?" Erika suggested.

Gianna shook her head. "Two minutes, tops."

Alex slapped Elio on the shoulder, continuing to tease him. Perhaps his jokes would have held more weight if he hadn't pulled out his own phone to show off *his* kids. He and Charley had two girls, and Charley mentioned Alex's desire to have another. Given the way Charley's hand surreptitiously slid to her stomach, Erika suspected that desire might already have been met.

Apparently, Alex insisted he wanted six, enough to outfit one line of a hockey team. Most women might have laughed that off, but Charley, a bestselling children's author, acted like that was a totally normal request.

After placing their drink orders, they chatted for another twenty minutes until the announcer broadcast the starting lineups for each team, followed by the National Anthem. Erika, Gianna, and Charley claimed the first row of box seats, while Elio and Alex sat behind them. The game—against Pittsburgh— was an exciting one, both teams in it to win it.

Erika had sent her parents pictures of the box seats shortly after her arrival, and her dad had let her know a few minutes ago that they'd seen her on TV. Apparently, the camera had spun to their box—not surprising, since Alex and Elio were two of the Rays' most popular former players—just as Blake scored the tying goal.

The goal was replayed on the jumbotron several times because it was such an incredible shot, Blake spinning around mid-shot in a way that seemed to defy gravity. The entire crowd in the arena had gotten to their feet to cheer, and the cameras had made sure to capture Alex and Elio's reactions.

From Dad's four exclamation marks following the words "I just saw you on TV," it was clear he was less impressed by the goal and more excited about seeing *her*. God, she loved her dad.

During the break between the second and third periods, Alex and Elio stood, hanging out by their personal bar, while she, Charley, and Gianna remained in their seats.

"So, what's new with you, Erika?" Gianna asked.

Erika started to offer a standard line. Something like "nothing much" or "same old, same old," but she stopped herself.

She'd never been the type of person who had a lot of friends. She didn't think she was unfriendly or anything like that. It was just that, for the majority of her young adult and adult life, she was always studying. Her social life had taken a massive backseat to her goals, so while other people were doing happy hours or club hopping, she was usually hunkered down in her apartment alone, her nose in a book, while living on takeout.

Blake was the first person since middle school who she actually called "best friend." Probably because they'd met at the right time. She had passed the board, survived her first year of residency, and for the first time since high school, Erika had time for a social life. And Blake was more than happy to share his with her, introducing her to his teammates and the other people in his circle of friends. His friends became hers, which worked well because she adored the same people he did.

But that also meant that now, she didn't really have anyone to talk to about Blake, who wasn't also Blake's friend.

She'd always been sorry that neither Gianna or Charley lived in Baltimore because she felt like the two of them could become very good girlfriends for her.

So, she took a chance.

"I slept with Blake."

Jesus. She probably could have torn that Band-Aid off slower.

Gianna and Charley's responses told her she'd chosen wisely. Both women smiled in genuine delight.

"Oh, I'm so glad!" Gianna enthused.

"You're perfect for each other," Charley added. "Alex and I were hoping the two of you would figure that out."

"The thing is…" Erika said, biting her lip.

Charley groaned. "Starting a sentence with 'the thing is' is never a good thing."

"It—the sex," Erika clarified, "only happened a few days ago, and since then, life has sort of kept us from talking about it. I got called into the hospital very early the morning after, and then Blake went on the road. We've been texting, but…"

"But?" Gianna prodded.

Erika shrugged. "It's hard as hell to interpret tone from texts, but all I'm getting from Blake's is that nothing has changed. It feels like we're still just friends."

"Do you want to be more than friends?" Charley asked.

Erika nodded immediately. "I thought I could handle a one-night stand with him. Thought it would be no problem to turn it off afterward."

Gianna crinkled her nose. "I'm not sure anyone, short of sociopaths, are capable of turning their feelings on and off like a faucet."

"The thing is, I don't do casual sex," Erika explained. "I don't really like being single. Lately, I've been feeling lonely. So I put myself out there, signed up for a couple online dating apps. I even started dating a guy. He turned out to be a horrible asshole, but I know what I'm hoping to find."

Charley frowned. "And you don't think Blake is it?"

"He doesn't want a relationship. Says marriage is something he'll consider after retiring from the game. He seems pretty damn attached to his bachelor status."

Gianna and Charley rolled their eyes.

"Guys are all the same," Charley said. "Total idiots when it comes to romance."

"And I think it's kind of worse for our guys—professional athletes," Gianna clarified. "I mean…it's not like they have to try too hard. The second they walk out of that locker room after a game, they can take their pick of women all clamoring for a night in their beds. Elio's retired, for God's sake, and even now, even tonight when we were walking into the arena, I swear no less than a dozen women approached him, flirting their asses off. And he was holding my hand!"

Charley nodded. "It's the same with Alex. Our guys have it too easy when it comes to women, and because they're simple-minded fools, they think they like it that way. Trust me. They don't. That's why they need us."

"Elio wasn't looking for love when we met. Of course, neither was I, for that matter," Gianna added. "I'd just gone through a painful breakup with a man I thought was the one. Then Mother Nature stepped in—"

"Mother Nature?" Erika asked.

Gianna smiled. "The two of us got trapped in his family's cabin in the Poconos during a blizzard. It gave us a lot of time to get to know one another and…I don't know. It felt like we both opened our eyes at the same time and saw what was standing right in front of us. Suddenly, I realized my ex had never been Mr. Right, and Elio figured out that puck bunnies would never be enough for him. Then Mother Nature stepped in again—"

"Another blizzard?" Charley joked.

Gianna shook her head. "The condom broke."

"Oh." Erika was aware hers and Charley's faces matched, and Gianna definitely found it funny, cracking up.

All three of them burst into laughter when Charley asked, "Mother Nature is in charge of condoms too?"

Gianna just shrugged, giggling.

Erika was so glad she'd started this conversation. It felt good to be able to talk to other women about stuff like this.

"Alex was the king of playboys back in his day," Charley said. "Blake looks like a choirboy in comparison."

"Sounds like Tank," Erika observed.

Charley nodded, giving her a look that proved she agreed with that assessment. "Mother Nature had nothing to do with converting my guy."

"What did?" Erika asked.

"Alcohol. The two of us got shit-faced at a friend's wedding in Vegas and eloped. We even enjoyed a drunken honeymoon in his hotel suite."

Erika's eyes widened. She knew Alex and Charley had grown up as neighbors, even playing on the same youth hockey leagues. She had always assumed they'd been childhood sweethearts. "Whoa."

"Right? I woke up the next morning hungover and looking for an annulment."

"*You* were looking for an annulment? Not Alex?" Gianna asked.

"That's the crazy part. Alex took me to that wedding as a favor to his sister. He wasn't looking for a relationship because he still considered himself God's gift to women."

Erika was struggling to follow Charley's story. "So why didn't the two of you get the annulment?"

"Alex refused at first, proclaiming he wanted *more honeymoon*." Charley grimaced. "I'm not proud to say that was a hard request to refuse because the sex..." She winked.

"The sex..." Gianna said with a happy sigh, glancing over her shoulder at Elio.

"Yeah," Erika agreed, perfectly aware that her days of being able to resist Blake's charms were over, now that she knew he wasn't one of those all-hat-and-no-cattle guys.

"I think the trick, Erika, isn't to listen to what Blake is saying. It's to watch what he's doing. I thought Alex wanted to stay married because the sex between us was great. But then he started showing me in a bunch of subtle, special ways that I was different from the other women in his past."

"You mean that even though Blake says he likes being a bachelor, that might not be true?" Erika hadn't considered that, but when she replayed the last few months, starting with the night they'd found Corky, she realized there had been quite a few changes in their relationship.

Blake had stopped bringing home puck bunnies, had stopped going to the pub after every win. He texted her more often, came home with sweet treats or a bottle of wine if she'd had a rough day at the hospital as a pick-me-up, and whenever he looked at her…

She felt beautiful.

Then she recalled the "masturbation lesson." The way he held her when she was scared or sad. The way he managed to cheer her up at her lowest points. The way he'd acted so jealous of Doug.

"Oh my God," Erika whispered. "Blake is my boyfriend! I think he has been for a while."

Gianna and Charley laughed, waving their hands in a jazz-hands cheer. "Yay!"

"So, I'll say it again," Charley said, leaning close to her. "The two of you are perfect for each other."

Erika enjoyed the third period of the game more than the first two—even though the game was a nailbiter—mainly because she was ready for what came after. She wasn't sure if Blake was prepared to admit what they were to each other, but that didn't matter. Because she was prepared to convince him. No wasn't an option here.

She was in love with her neighbor, her best friend, Blake.

And she couldn't wait to tell him.

Unfortunately, Murphy's Law wasn't finished kicking her around just yet. Five minutes before the final buzzer, the score was tied once more, and Pittsburgh had a power play. Erika wasn't sure she'd taken a breath in the last thirty seconds as the opposing team fired off three shots, almost consecutively. Mercifully, Coulton saved every single one.

Just before the power play ended, Erika's phone buzzed with an incoming call. She frowned when she saw her mom's name on the screen. Her parents knew she was at the game.

She started to let it go to voicemail, but then she thought better of it. Her parents had met and married late in life, which was one of the reasons she was an only child. Mom had been forty-five when she had Erika, her dad nearly fifty. With them now in their late seventies, Erika couldn't in good conscience ignore their phone call, even if she did suspect it was a butt dial.

"Mom?" she said, placing one finger in her ear as she rose from her seat. She could hear her mom talking but couldn't make out what she was saying.

"Wait a second while I get to where I can hear you." It was too loud in the arena, so she made her way out of the box to the corridor, where it was quieter. "That's better. Is everything okay?"

Her mom was speaking in a hushed tone. "I'm upstairs because your dad didn't want me to call you."

Erika didn't like Mom's anxious tone. "What's wrong?"

"He forgot tomorrow was trash day, so during the last break in the game, he went to drag the garbage can to the street. It was icy and he slipped, fell off the curb, and twisted his ankle."

"Is he alright? Did he break anything?" Erika knew her father, the most stoic man on the planet, would act fine even if he wasn't.

"It's very swollen. I told him we should go to the ER, but the truth is I'm not sure he can get to the car on his own, and I'm not strong enough to help." Mom was a petite five-two to her dad's hulking six-foot frame.

Erika didn't even bother suggesting Mom call an ambulance because she knew hell would freeze over before her dad admitted to needing one. "I'll come over and try to convince him to go to the hospital. If it's a fracture, he'll need X-rays."

"That's what I told him, but he swears he's fine with just icing it in his recliner. He didn't want me to call because you're at the game, but I'm worried."

"I'm going to leave now. The game is still going, so I shouldn't have to fight too much traffic. Hopefully, I'll be there in twenty, twenty-five minutes. Make sure he doesn't try to walk on that ankle."

"I will. Thank you, Erika." Mom hung up, and Erika returned to the box to grab her coat and purse.

"I have to go. Emergency with my dad. He took a tumble," she said to the two couples.

"Is he okay?" Alex asked.

"Swollen ankle, but he's being a stubborn old coot, so I'm making a house call," she said, a weak attempt at a joke to mask the fact she was concerned. "If everything is okay, I'll meet you at the pub later. If he needs to go to the hospital, I'm afraid I'll miss the after-party." Erika spared a quick glance at the score-board. "The Rays scored?"

"Blake fired one in about ten seconds after you stepped out," Elio said.

She grimaced. "Figures. Can you tell Blake I'm sorry to bail? I'll text him too."

Charley reached out and gave her a hug. "We'll tell him. Go take care of your dad. Hope to see you soon, Erika."

"Same," Erika replied, hugging Alex, Gianna, and Elio before heading out. From the roar that greeted her the second she hit the stairs, she could tell the Rays had scored again. And she'd missed it...*again.*

Once she made it to the concourse level, she headed toward the exit.

"You're leaving?"

Erika turned around, surprised to discover it was Mindy, emerging from a lower level, headed toward the bathroom.

"Yeah. Family emergency."

"Oh. So I guess you're going to miss the after-party."

"Probably." She was annoyed that Mindy wasn't even trying to hide her delight over Erika's departure.

"The celebration at the pub is going to be off the hook," Mindy continued. "The Rays pulled out a major upset, and the way Blake scored those last two goals…magic."

Shit, Erika thought. She'd missed seeing him score both those goals.

"I really do need to run." Erika tried to ignore the unwanted jealousy she felt. Blake appeared to have lost interest in Mindy, but unfortunately, Erika was still insecure enough about her own place in his life that she was worried.

She tried to shake those feelings off as she headed to the parking garage. On the way, she typed out a quick text.

> Dad fell and twisted his ankle. Had to leave early. Congratulations on the game. It was a brilliant win.

She'd search for highlights on her phone to watch Blake's goals.

> Sorry I can't celebrate with you. Enjoy your night with the gang, and thanks again for the tickets. Felt very bougie sitting in that box.

She considered adding a champagne emoji, but in the end, she opted for something simpler and more appropriate.

> xoxo

CHAPTER THIRTEEN

BLAKE LATHERED HIS FACE, wetting his razor. He was out of bed a little earlier than usual this morning, but that was on purpose. He was going to see Erika today—within the next twenty minutes, even if he had to move heaven and fucking earth to make it happen.

He'd been disappointed and worried when he'd seen her texts last night after the game. Blake had spent a lot of time with her parents, who were totally awesome, so he'd been concerned about her dad. The guy was turning eighty on his next birthday, so Blake didn't blame Erika for hightailing it out of the game to check on him.

He'd texted her, asking her to keep him in the loop, and she had, texting him several more times during the night.

She had convinced the old guy to go to the hospital for X-rays, which was a good thing because he *had* fractured his ankle. Unfortunately, that meant they'd spent several hours in the ER while he was fitted for a boot, after which, Erika had taken her parents home to get her dad settled.

Blake had no idea what time she finally made it home. He'd tried to stay awake, listening for her, but he'd fallen asleep some-time after three a.m. on the couch with Corky.

He'd also spent too much of the night analyzing those x's and o's she'd texted him, perfectly aware she had never used that sign-off before.

It was ridiculous how those two letters had taken him from dark to light in one-point-four seconds. He'd read her text about leaving the game early, and while he'd been concerned about her dad, there was a small part of him that worried perhaps she was using her parents as an excuse to avoid him.

Then he'd seen the *xoxo*, and something that felt very much like hope erased that fear completely. Between that and scoring the goals, he'd felt ten feet tall and bulletproof as he celebrated the win with old friends and his teammates.

Spending time with Elio, Alex, and their wives at Pat's Pub had been a great boost for his confidence as Charley and Gianna both expressed how much they liked Erika, and how a man would have to be a fool not to snatch up a woman like her. They'd become less and less obvious about their matchmaking attempts as the night progressed, until Blake started to suspect Erika had said something to them.

He grinned when he heard a knock on his door. Despite her late night, it appeared Erika was just as anxious to see him as he was her.

"Come in. It's unlocked," he yelled from the bathroom, when he didn't hear the door open.

"Since when do we knock?" he muttered to himself, relieved when he heard footsteps coming down the hall.

"I'll be out in a minute," he said, scraping the razor over his jaw. "Just need to finish shaving."

He heard her and Corky moving around the bedroom, Erika no doubt playing with the puppy while she waited.

Grabbing the toothpaste, he brushed his teeth quickly because he'd already decided the second he went out there, he was kissing his girl senseless until there was no question between them that she was his.

Rinsing out his mouth, he ran his fingers through his wet

hair, still wearing just the towel he'd wrapped around his hips after climbing out of the shower.

He grinned, deciding not to lead with the kiss.

Nope. He had a better idea how to get this party started.

Walking into his bedroom, he pulled the towel off and dropped it to the floor just as he looked up.

He scowled.

Because it wasn't Erika waiting for him, playing with Corky.

It was Mindy.

Naked and tied to his bed.

What the *fuck*?

Blake frowned, thinking he'd spoken his thoughts aloud… until he realized he'd heard them in a female voice.

He turned, panicking when he saw it was Erika who'd asked the question. Then he recognized exactly what Erika was seeing from her vantage point in the doorway to his bedroom.

"Shit," he cursed, bending down to retrieve his towel, covering himself with it before turning back to Mindy. "I don't know what the fuck you're doing here, but get dressed!"

Mindy looked equal parts chagrinned and embarrassed. "Can you untie me?"

Jesus Christ!

Blake walked over to the bed, hastily loosening the knots on her wrists, careful to keep his eyes on Erika. He was terrified she'd make a run for it.

Mercifully, she stayed put, though that felt like a small comfort, considering the expression on her face was pure murder.

How the fuck was he going to explain this?

Once Mindy was free, Blake turned away from her, gripping Erika's elbow and guiding her down the hallway. When they were in the living room, he placed himself between her and the door, ready to tackle her if she tried to make a break for it.

"Erik," he said. "I didn't know she was here."

Erika frowned. "She's tied up."

He hadn't told her about Mindy's ridiculous talent because he took enough teasing from her about the puck bunny.

"It's her party trick."

Erika snorted. "Of course it is. Might be a neater trick if she could *untie* herself too," she muttered.

Blake couldn't quite interpret that response. It sounded not only like she believed him…but like she was amused.

That couldn't be right. Could it?

Before he could test that theory, Mindy came down the hall.

"Sorry, Blake," she said, glancing from him to Erika and back again. "Last night's game was awesome. So I thought I'd surprise you."

"You did," he murmured.

Mindy laughed humorlessly. "Yeah. Well, I guess I'll leave you guys to…" She waved her hand, gesturing to him and Erika. "Whatever this is. Bye, Erika."

Wow. Mindy finally got Erika's name right. Not that Blake expected that to help him get out of this predicament.

Erika lifted her hand. "Bye, Mandy."

Tou-fucking-ché.

Blake had to bite his lip not to laugh out loud.

The second the door closed behind Mindy, Blake started talking. "Erika, I swear to you—"

"Blake," she started.

Panic was his overriding every other emotion as the stress of the past few days caught up with him. Because even if he hadn't said the words, she had to fucking know how he felt about her. He threw his hands in the air. "Goddammit! You don't *really* think I would bring Mindy back here, would sleep with her after what you and I—"

"I don't," she interjected loudly, cutting his tirade short. "I know you wouldn't do that."

For the first time since seeing Mindy in his bed, Blake managed to take a full breath. "You do?"

She nodded. "Of course I do."

Her eyes were softer now, the anger he'd seen in his bedroom completely gone. Suddenly it occurred to him maybe that ire wasn't directed at him but at Mindy. It gave him the courage to take a step closer.

"God, I missed you," he whispered.

His confession made her smile, which made his heart beat faster.

"I missed you too," she admitted. "So much."

With those words, Blake closed the distance between them, reaching out to wrap his arms around her. The smell of her—that sweet white peach—worked like a goddamn aphrodisiac and had him hard in an instant.

He ignored it. Last time they were together, he let his libido take charge. This time, he was making sure they said everything that needed to be said. He wasn't leaving anything to chance, wasn't willing to let there be any misunderstandings.

"Erik, I need you to know what this is."

She grinned. "I already do."

His brows furrowed. "You do?"

She nodded. "Yep."

He waited for her to elaborate…but she didn't.

Not good enough. He needed to say it. Needed to hear the words from her.

"So you know you're my girlfriend? You know that I'm so fucking in love with you, I can't see straight? You know that before the day is out, we're going to have to flip a coin to see whose apartment we're both living in together?"

She laughed. "You want to live together?"

"*That* was what you took from all that?"

Erika snaked her arms around his shoulders. "I already knew the rest. I'm your girlfriend. And…" She blushed. Fuck, he loved it when she blushed. "I love you too."

Blake blew out a long, slow breath as every drop of tension flowed from his body. He pressed his forehead against hers, closing his eyes. "Thank God," he breathed, remaining there for a moment, soaking in how good it felt to have her in his arms like this, with all the walls down, all the secrets told.

When he lifted his head, he gave her a soft kiss on the cheek. "And to answer your question, yes, we're living together. Because I plan to spend every single night I'm home in the same damn bed as you. And on the nights when I'm on the road, we're going to FaceTime and sext our asses off. Which reminds me…" He narrowed his eyes. "You're going to have to up your texting game when I'm gone, Erik. You ghosted me one whole day during this last trip and—"

"I had food poisoning."

He reared back. "What?"

Erika gave him a guilty grimace. "I grabbed a sandwich from one of the vending machines at work…"

She stumbled when he placed his hands on his hips.

"And?" he asked, not bothering to hide his annoyed tone.

"And I got food poisoning. Spent one whole day hugging the toilet. By the way, I'm giving Ashley a raise on her hourly rate. That girl was a lifesaver."

"I agree on the raise. Ashley is amazing." Then, he grinned. "Well, I guess that just proves we have no choice but to live together. Clearly, you need me around full-time to make sure you're eating right."

Erika drew one finger down the center of his bare chest. "You know…" she drawled, her tone pure seduction. "I *am* kinda hungry right now."

"Is that right?" he replied, loving the hell out of where her head was.

She nodded. "Starving, actually." Her fingers made their way over his stomach, stopping at where the bath towel was hanging low around his hips.

"Should I make us some scrambled eggs?" he teased.

She shook her head. "No."

"Toast?"

She shook her head again, her fingers slipping underneath the towel. "It's not that kind of hunger."

"Oh, gotcha." He tried not to chuckle when he said, "You want bacon."

Erika laughed, and he joined her, though it was short-lived when she ripped the towel off. To be honest, it was a miracle the thing stayed on, considering the tent his cock had pitched beneath the soft material.

He grunted when Erika wasted no time grasping his cock, running her hand up and down with a firm grip that was already testing his control.

Blake placed his hand over hers, slowing her pace as he leaned toward her, giving her a long, wet, hard kiss.

By the time they parted, her breathing was as labored as his.

Blake's lips were by her ear when he said, "Take off your clothes, dirty girl."

She released his cock. He missed her hand instantly, so when she didn't move quickly enough, shrugging off her hoodie, he took over.

She shook her head, grinning widely when he stripped off her bra in record time. "You are ridiculously good at that," she said, raising one accusatory eyebrow.

Blake may have suffered a few concussions during the course of his career, but he hadn't been hit on the head enough that he'd make a joke about having lots of practice in that particular area.

Besides, it was clear Erika already knew exactly why he was well-versed in snapping bra hooks free.

He brushed her fingers away, unfastening her jeans, which he shoved down to her ankles along with her panties. That was when he realized she'd crossed the hall to his place barefoot. She hadn't bothered with shoes, which—while not an uncommon thing— told him just how anxious she'd been to see him this morning.

Once she was naked, Erika started to reach for his dick again, but he moved faster. Flipping their positions, he pushed her until her back was pressed against his living room wall. He kissed her again, but this time, he was unable to make it soft or gentle or even fucking sweet.

Erika wasn't the only one who was hungry. The last few days had been hell on him—emotionally and physically.

Now that they'd said what needed to be said, his body was demanding its own satisfaction.

Erika's fingers pushed through his hair, her fists closing around it. She was using that tight grip to keep his lips on hers. She didn't need to expend the effort. He wasn't going anywhere any time soon.

Their tongues stroked, and Erika whimpered when he nipped at her lower lip. His cock brushed against her bare stomach as she pressed her hips closer, fighting to take even more.

Then, before she could read his intention, he knelt before her, throwing one of her legs over his shoulder, running his tongue over her clit, loving the way she gasped—the perfect blend of surprise and desire.

"Blake," she breathed. "God."

He loved the way she said his name, the way her hands clawed at the wall behind her as he teased her clit with his tongue and his teeth.

"Please," she begged.

"More," he demanded. She was going to beg a lot more. "Beg me, dirty girl."

"Blake!" There was so much need in her tone. He liked it. A lot.

"Better," he murmured against her pussy.

She huffed out a breathy laugh, her body twitching when he added his fingers to the game, circling her opening, coating his finger with her arousal before sliding back until he found her anus.

She jerked hard enough that he had to pull away. Glancing at her flushed face, he winked as he pushed just the tip of his finger into that tight hole.

Erika threw her head back, lightly banging it on the wall behind her. He wiggled his finger for a moment, before returning his attention to her clit, stroking it harder and faster, driving her closer and closer to the edge.

"More. I need you inside me," she said, her gaze never leaving his. "So fucking much. These last few days... Please don't tease me. I don't think I can—"

She stopped when he rose rapidly, her pleas mimicking his own feelings, his own strung-out needs.

Drawing out the teasing and building the anticipation were games they could play later.

They had a lifetime, after all.

The old Blake might have panicked at the thought of forever with one woman, but Erika's Blake...he was here. For. It.

He gripped her ass, using that hold to lift her.

"Wrap your legs around my waist," he demanded.

Erika was halfway there before he finished telling her what he wanted, her arms encircling his neck as he used the wall at her back to hold her one-handed, moving the other to guide his cock—

Fuck.

His *uncovered* cock.

Blake stilled, glancing down the hallway of his apartment, toward his bedroom. Where his stash of condoms were.

"I get the birth control shot," she said, reading his thoughts.

He frowned. Was she saying... "I'm clean," he swore.

She nodded, her eyes heavy with a need that told him she didn't want to make that trip down the hall any more than he did. "I trust you, Blake," she whispered. "Just us this time. Nothing between."

He kissed her again, because Jesus, every word out of her mouth felt like the most beautiful song he'd ever heard. As they kissed, he ran the head of his cock along her slit, her very wet, very hot slit.

Then, he pushed inside and found heaven.

He entered her with one hard, fast, no-holds-barred thrust that pushed her up the wall as she cried out and—*fuck him*—came. Immediately.

Her pussy constricted hard, squeezing him so tightly he saw stars. He held still, gritting his teeth painfully until her orgasm wavered, then faded.

They were nowhere near done.

"More will kill me," she murmured, her forehead pressed to his shoulder.

Blake didn't realize he'd spoken aloud. Unfortunately, he needed this—her—too much, so he let go of his hard-won control and took her, claimed her.

"Mine," he growled in her ear, as he fucked her with a force he'd never used with another woman. Erika met him blow for blow, her hips moving in time with his thrusts, driving him deeper.

"Yes!" she cried out, telling him she was almost there again. He reached between them and delivered the knock-out punch, pinching her clit.

Erika keened, her eyes closed as her body shook. Blake held her tightly, aware that if he wasn't, she'd be sliding down the wall, her bones turned to jelly.

This time, he didn't hold still as she came back to herself. He continued to shift inside her, a slow in, a slower out, drawing out her orgasm as she shook in his arms.

It was a full minute before Erika regained her wits, opened her eyes, and realized he was still hard, still inside her.

"Blake," she said, her voice hoarse from her cries.

"More," he repeated.

This time she didn't argue, didn't offer a single bit of resistance when he lowered her legs and twisted her until she faced away from him. Then he guided her toward the couch, pushing her face down over one arm.

She jolted when he slapped her ass, more a light tap than something painful. He had intended to leave it there, but the shameless flirt wiggled her ass, so he gave her a couple more, these with more force.

Erika glanced over her shoulder, her cheeks still flushed from her first two orgasms. "Don't tease me with a good time."

He laughed at her joke, even as his body ached for completion.

"Later," he promised, before guiding his cock to her opening and slamming inside once more.

Erika found her second wind fast, lifting her hips in time, breathlessly begging him. "Deeper. Harder. God, Blake! So good."

Her words as much as her actions pushed him to the cliff, and this time he gave in, jumping into the abyss, shocked and thrilled when Erika went over with him.

He filled her with his come—wondering how long he should wait to propose and how much time he had to let pass before he asked her to stop getting the birth control shot. Now that he had her, he wanted it all. He was going to be greedy and demanding, God help his woman.

The two of them remained there, connected, quiet except for their breathing, which slowed as they managed to calm their racing hearts.

He really should pull out, but there was something very tempting about keeping his come inside her, even though he knew nothing would take root.

Now that he'd imagined Erika pregnant, it was all he could think about.

Finally, the decision to stay buried within her was taken away from him. Blake withdrew, he and Erika laughing, as Corky hopped on the couch. Erika's head was still pressed against the cushion, something the cute puppy took advantage of as Corky started licking her face.

"Corky." Erika lifted a clumsy hand to try to pet the adorable puppy demanding affection.

Blake reached down, helping Erika upright, steadying her until she found her strength.

"It's still early," he said. "What do you say we crawl back into bed for an hour or so?"

"That sounds perfect." Erika led the way to his bedroom, standing in front of him while he wrapped his arms around her from behind, his hands gently stroking her stomach.

She looked at the bed, pure mischievous in her gaze when she glanced over her shoulder. "Do I need to learn any fancy bedroom party tricks to keep you interested?"

He groaned. It was too damn soon to joke about Mindy's little show. "No. You don't." Victor's words from the plane drifted back to him. "When you're tied up in my bed, I'm going to be the one tightening the ropes."

He didn't miss Erika's slight intake of breath. Soooo…she liked the idea of bondage. Just when he thought he couldn't love her any more.

Then he considered all the ways he wanted to bind this woman to him.

"That's not the only way I'm going to tie you up," he said, his lips sliding along the side of her neck as he spoke.

"Do tell," she whispered.

"I'm going to drag your sweet ass in front of an altar and tie us together with vows and rings too."

Erika hummed. "I like the sound of that."

"Then I'm going to go for the hat trick," he continued. "Husband. Wife… Parents."

Erika twisted in his arms. "You want babies?"

"Hell yeah. And not just for me. Corky needs siblings."

She laughed. "I guess she has sort of been our practice kid."

"And we've been nailing it," he pointed out.

"Except for that time I lost her," Erika said, grinning widely.

"Yeah," he agreed, chuckling. "Except for that time. So what do you say, Erik? Should we go ahead and claim it all—marriage, babies, forever? Because it seems like that kind of win deserves a victory dance." He wiggled his eyebrows as he tilted his head toward the bed.

Erika shook her head, smiling. "You have no restraint, Balakay. And I love that about you."

Be sure to check out the rest of the Stingrays Hockey series, coming soon!

Resist (March 2025) - Coulton's story

Rematch (July 2025) - Preston's story

Release (January 2026) - Tank's story

Reclaim (June 2026) - Victor's story

ABOUT THE AUTHOR

Virginia native Mari Carr is a New York Times and USA TODAY bestseller of contemporary romance novels. With over three million copies of her books sold, Mari was the winner of the Romance Writers of America's Passionate Plume award for her novella, Erotic Research. She has over a hundred published works, including her popular Wild Irish and Italian Stallions books, along with the Trinity Masters series she writes with Lila Dubois.

Follow Mari:
www.maricarr.com
mari@maricarr.com

Join her newsletter so you don't miss new releases and for exclusive subscriber-only content.